Vanilla Twist

A *Walk on the Wild Side* Novel
Sequel to *Vanilla on Top*

C.J. Ellisson

Red Hot Publishing
P.O. BOX 651193, STERLING VA, 20165-1193

First Print Edition March 2014

Copyright 2014 C.J. Ellisson, All Rights Reserved

Edited by Tina Winograd
Cover Design by Kim Killion, HotDamnDesigns.com

ISBN 9781938601262

PUBLISHER'S NOTE
This is a work of fiction. Names, characters, places, and incidents are either the products of the author's imagination or are used fictitiously, and any resemblance to actual persons, living or dead, business establishments, events, or locales is entirely coincidental.

For Peter, my very own Tony.

Acknowledgements

I know I'm always thanking my readers in this section, but honestly, if it wasn't for all of you I'd never be where I am today. I'm living the dream so many writers aspire to, and I have the support of my readers to thank for it. You lift me up when I'm feeling down, you offer comments and suggestions on Facebook when my health issues threaten to overwhelm me yet again, and you laugh at my attempts at humor. Thank you.

My alpha readers stepped up to the plate on this manuscript. Once again, I'd taken on too much in my personal and work life and worked all the way to the wire on this novel. You ladies read and offered feedback faster than I could have ever expected. Big, BIG thanks to **Sandy Schairer**, **Katrina Hough**, **Dea Jones**, **Patricia Statham**, **Kim Lapp**, **Danielle Nicholson**, **Cheryl Cape**, **Laura Ward**, **Kim Engstrom**, **Melissa Nelson**, **Teri Zuwala**, **Samantha Cudworth**, **Peggy Ptacek**, **Andrea Genovesi**, **Chelly Pazdan**, **Wendy Higgins**, **Tara Horn**, and **Anna Cade**. Writing is often a solitary journey and I appreciate your friendship and support more than you could ever know. Thanks again for being a part of the creative process with me.

Thank you, Tina Winograd, for consistently being an editor who understands my vision and respects it, and for always improving my prose. You rock, girlfriend. I had a new proof reader on this book, Angela King, recommended to me by one of my loyal readers, Caren King. Thank you for working on a tight deadline with a sharp eye, you did a great job!

As always, the biggest thanks goes to my husband, Pete. I really appreciate you agreeing to be my fully-clothed, posable fuck-dummy when I needed to "picture" a scene, and for patiently waiting while I wrote the scene immediately.

Note From the Author

This book was a long time coming, and I apologize for the delay. I promise you won't have to wait another year for the final installment of Tony and Heather's story, *Vanilla Spice*. I'd always plotted this as a three book series, but my former publisher wanted three different couples, hence Carla's story that came out in between the two *Vanilla* books. To clear up any confusion, *Avoiding Mr. Right* and *Loving Ms. Wrong* (Novella, eBook only, March 2014) take place **after** all three of Heather and Tony's books.

Chapter One

Heather

"Heather?" A warm hand slides over my hip. Soft, moist lips press against one shoulder. "It's Monday. You've got work today."

I resist the urge to snuggle under the covers and spend the rest of the day like the weekend—naked and sweaty. Tony's hips move behind mine, his arousal stroking between the cheeks of my ass. His enthusiasm isn't making me want to get out of bed, either.

"What time is it?" I struggle to rise to examine the clock.

Tony holds me firmly in place. "A little before six. You've got plenty of time." His fingers dig into my hip, guiding them in a slow motion while he thrusts softly against me. "I don't need to be in Jersey until later." He relaxes his grasp, perhaps drawing out his own anticipation. "Excited about starting your new job?"

Unsurprisingly, my new job is the furthest thing from my mind at the moment. "Job?" My voice sounds rough with sleep. "You really want to talk about work?"

His masculine chuckle warms the skin of my back. He curves closer, pressing his upper body firmly along my spine. "You're right. My bad. I want you focused on what you're feeling." Tony places lingering kisses up my neck, nibbling at the skin below my jaw.

My eyes fly open as he sucks where his teeth grazed me. "Hey! Not so hard. I need to look professional."

Tony releases the suction. "Yes, ma'am." He kisses me again, ending with a light lick. "Wouldn't want that."

I squirm, pressing myself toward his cock. The idea of him wanting to mark me, to let the world know I'm taken, stirs something primal within me. Makes me want to mark him, too. Although working on his apartment doesn't allow him much exposure to the dating public.

And really, am I that type of girl? I'm close to thirty. I should be past having to mark my man. *My man.* That has a nice ring to it. Would he like me to brand him with a love bite? Perhaps I could leave one where only he can see it.

That would be sexy as well as fun. I'll do it. The moment I can think clearly and get a chance.

The hand on my hip curves inward, questing fingers slip between my thighs.

His husky voice whispers in my ear, "I can think of a terrific way to start your day."

I gasp as he finds my clit, sliding two fingers to rub gently.

"It'll be a great stress reliever, too. You'll start your new job well-rested and relaxed."

Considering the amount of hours I was awake last night and panting under his hard body, I doubt I'll be too rested. But who the hell cares? I roll onto my back and spread my thighs. This feels too good to ignore.

I stifle a yawn and push my hips up to meet his hand. "What do you have in mind, mister?"

The desire glowing in his light brown eyes leaves me reeling. I can still hardly believe how things worked out last week. Tony, waiting for me in my apartment building's lobby when I'd thought I'd messed things up for good. Life is getting better and better by the day.

He leans in to kiss me, his morning scruff tickling my chin. Tony's mouth meets mine and a shudder races down my frame. God, he's simply delicious. And all mine.

He pulls back and nips my bottom lip. "Would you like hard and fast or slow and leisurely?"

An idea comes to me. I push him onto his back and straddle his hips. "I'll let you know." I reach down and clasp his length, guiding him inside me.

Tony wastes no time and thrusts his hips up to meet mine, his hands grabbing both breasts. "That's it, baby. Ride me. I love when you take what you want."

His words excite me further. In past relationships I never considered being sexually aggressive, always content to accept whatever was offered. But this man, he brings out the sex kitten in me. I want to shock him. I want to leave him guessing. I want him always craving more—of me.

I angle my hips and rub forward and back, grinding my mound on his pelvic bone to get the pressure I crave. Hot palms cup my small breasts, squeezing and kneading a moment before agile fingers seek out my nipples. A sharp twist of the aroused peaks pulls a gasp from me.

"Look at me," he says. I stare down into his expressive eyes. "I want to see all of you when you come."

He releases one breast and maneuvers his hand between us, his thumb stroking right where I need it.

"Yesss... That feels so good..." My eyes drift close and he tweaks my nipple hard, drawing my attention back to his gaze.

"Don't look away. Be in the moment with me."

His heart shines in his eyes, the emotion deep and strong. The raw edge of his hunger weaves an impassioned spell, encasing us both. This incredible man never fails to surprise me.

"Faster," I gasp. "I'm close."

Pressure builds inside as I bump and grind. His hips rise up to meet mine, pounding deep inside me. The slap of heated flesh rings loud in the quiet room, the only other sound our panting breaths.

"That's it..." A long low keening of sound spills from my lips as I falter in my rhythm. Tony increases his pace, pushing me over the edge into oblivion. His grip on my breast becomes rough, merging a tinge of pain with my release.

The electric tingle of orgasm lights inside me, curving my back and bringing my face near his. I latch my mouth onto his as he erupts, his shout of pleasure causing his teeth to clank against mine. His hands leave my clit and breast to grab my hips, slamming me down on him while his orgasm wracks his frame.

After a few gasping breaths we settle, his hands gentling and rising to soothe along my spine. His voice sounds mellow and satiated. "What a great way to start the day."

A sigh escapes me as I nuzzle near his neck. "You said it."

The enticing aroma of fresh bagels fills my head as I slowly spin to examine my new office space. The company's former CFO and my boss, Harvey, cleared out his stuff last week when the board pushed his retirement. The room has been cleaned vigorously by the building's janitorial staff and now awaits me to make it my own. Wonder and awe swell inside my chest.

This is it, girlfriend. You've made it to the top!

When I started at Parkerson right out of college I had no idea, in just shy of seven years, I'd be the youngest member the board has ever accepted into its ranks, *and* the only woman, to boot.

A throat clears behind me and I turn to see a huge bouquet of flowers dwarfing the woman who holds their glass vase. "These came for you." Melissa, one of the receptionists, strides across the room to set the arrangement on a sideboard near my new desk. "They arrived special order—by messenger." She glances at her wrist. "I don't think we've ever had flowers arrive before eight a.m."

Warmth floods my face. There's only one person I know in my life who'd do something so extravagant. Melissa fusses with the flowers a moment before reaching for the card. Without opening it, she hands the small envelope to me in passing, her eyebrows raised. "As if the simple fact the exotic blooms outshine any rose isn't enough, *your* admirer wanted to make sure the arrangement arrived bright and early, too."

I nod my thanks, too overwhelmed with emotion to speak. I clutch the tiny card to my chest, scurrying to the lush flowers to take a deep breath of their heady fragrance. I fan my heated cheeks with the card and stare at the artfully arranged blossoms. Vibrant yellows, oranges and reds stand out like flames among smaller white flowers with tiny black centers. I have no idea what any of them are called, but I'll be searching the Internet later when I take a break.

Such luxury could only come from Tony. I make my way to the deep leather seat behind my desk and sit, eager to see what he wrote on the card.

Go get 'em, tiger!
Wishing you the best in your new position,
Tony

A huge smile spreads across my face. Considering the wake-up I received this morning, I never expected him to send flowers, too.

I picture Tony's relaxed, boxer-brief clad physique leaning against my kitchen counter this morning. His defined abs tightened when he laughed at something silly I said, distracting me yet again. Only this time I over-filled my coffee cup while I was staring. Which of course led to more laughter from my new lover.

A shiver runs through me as I recall our weekend lovemaking. There was no hesitancy between us as we casually traded control and assertiveness with each sexual encounter. In my wildest dreams I never expected a man as successful and handsome as Tony would want me.

I rummage around in my purse, looking for my cell phone, impulsively deciding to call him. After all, work hours haven't officially started yet.

He answers, a teasing note in his voice. "Hey. Didn't expect to hear from you so early."

"I just bet! Your flowers arrived. They're stunning, thank you."

"Good. I'm glad you like them." He hesitates for a second and my heart hitches in my chest. Does he regret sending them? Have I made too big of a deal over something he considers small? I hate this new relationship crap and not knowing what I should say or do. "So... I opened your bedside drawer a few minutes ago. Looking for a nail file..."

My stuttering heart lurches to a stop. Oh. My. God. Please don't tell me he's found the leather cock ring and vibrator I bought online two weeks ago after we met. It was my first attempt to buy something sexy and adventurous and later I felt too awkward to even bring them out. I should have hid the darn things in my closet.

His voice deepens, and my nipples tighten at the exact tone he used in my ear this morning. "Let's just say I found two un-opened items I'd like to... explore with you."

A blush heats my face. Of course he found the sex toys. "Really? Er... um... I..."

He laughs, the masculine sound tickling all the way from my ear to my privates. "You did buy them for us, right? I'm not wrong in thinking they're new since they're still in the plastic packaging?" I hear the shift of a drawer opening and picture him rummaging through my bedside table once more and handling the risqué purchases. "I'll try to contain my jealousy if they were for another guy, but I won't make any guarantees."

"No! I... er... I did buy them with you in mind. I just..."

"Wasn't sure when to spring them on me?" There's a light teasing to his voice. God, I'm so mortified right now I wish I could die.

I channel my inner vixen, willing my sexual confidence of the past weekend to come out. I can do this. I can be the sexy woman who made love to Tony yesterday and screamed his name at the top of my lungs. "Yes, you're exactly right." I lower my voice, cognizant

I'm at work and can't do anything about the emotions and sexual cravings this conversation is stirring up. "I bet the black leather will look magnificent around your..."

A meeting reminder pops up on my computer screen, pulling me from my teasing. I have to meet with Oliver and Grant, head of sales, at two this afternoon. What a nice reminder—*not*—that I've got a job to do.

"Yes?" Tony's eager voice jars me back to the call. "You were saying? Around what?"

I chuckle, sexual awareness of the moment and how he's reacting to me like a balm to my mortification. "You know where it belongs. I'm looking forward to trying it, too. But I've got to go. You're getting me so wrapped up in thinking about sex I'll mess up my first day."

A heavy sigh reaches me. "Wouldn't want that, would we? Hold those thoughts for tonight. You shouldn't work too late on your first day. They'll expect it all the time."

I lean back in my chair, the softness cushioning my spine. "True. What are you doing today?"

"I'm leaving for Hoboken in a few minutes to work on dry wall, then I'll be back this way mid-afternoon for a meeting at Apollo. They want help on transitioning deals."

Apprehension fills me when I think of him quitting his job last week. Will he be happy with this new change in his life?

Admit it. What you're really worried about is if he will stay happy with you or grow bored.

I shake the self-doubting ruminations from my head. No one can predict the future. It's best to enjoy what we have in the here and now.

A tentative knock sounds at my door. I glance up to see an attractive woman in conservative clothing. She has long blond highlighted hair pulled back severely in a low ponytail and her clear green eyes look at me hopefully, not much makeup needed to enhance their stunning color. The trim woman appears older than me, perhaps in her mid-to-late thirties.

"I've got to go," I say into my cell. "We'll talk later?"

"Sure. Dinner tonight to celebrate your first day?"

Warmth heats my cheeks as the woman watches me with patience. "Sounds good. Bye." I hang up and smile. "Hi," I say to the new arrival. "Can I help you?"

The woman steps into the room, hand extended. "I'm Tammy. I've been assigned to help you until you hire your own assistant."

I grasp her offered hand and shake. "Nice to meet you." I release my hold and gesture to an open seat. "Please, tell me a little about yourself."

She smiles self-consciously and smoothes a non-existent loose hair behind an ear. "Not much to tell, really. I've worked at Parkerson for about two years."

"What department were you in?"

Tammy wrinkles her button nose. "Ad design."

"Not your favorite, I presume?"

"It wasn't bad. Not great, either. My degree is in marketing with a minor in business. I've worked for banks and pharmaceutical companies. Decided a change was in order a few years ago." She shrugs. "The art end of advertising isn't where I'd hoped to specialize." Her eyes fill with an eager light. "I immediately volunteered when I heard you'd need someone while you settled in."

"Great. I could sure use a hand today." I stand and motion toward the expanse of boxes hauled in from my old office. "Want to help me unload and organize? It's not fun. But we have to start somewhere."

With a nod and a shared smile, we set to work. She even helps me hang the framed prints I brought from home. Including them in my new office space reminds me of two passions: photography and the way I felt when I took the pictures, and Tony, the man who bought me a new camera to encourage something I love that's just for me. As far as beginnings go, today could have been much worse.

Tammy leaves for lunch around noon and I grab my phone, eager to see if Tony's texted me. I made a conscious effort not to check while Tammy and I were unpacking—it was difficult to resist digging my phone out every ten minutes. He's left two messages since our call this morning.

His first one, *Can't get that cock ring out of my head,* came in shortly after nine a.m.

My inner voice chimes in with the obvious, *You've got it bad, girlfriend.*

Yeah—and so what if I do? After the assholes I've dated, is it any wonder I'm still in shock over how great Tony is?

I scroll down through my texts to see he tried me again two hours later.

Feel like anything in particular tonight for dinner?

My heart beats faster, the desire to dial his cell feels like a baby bird attempting first flight is trapped in my chest. I take a deep breath to calm down. I don't want to appear too eager, right? Then again, he has texted me twice without me responding so I should be okay if I call him. Or maybe I should text him. That's always safer.

I hate all this uncertainty. All these damn games we play in relationships. Don't look too eager, don't be too available, don't say *I love you* first. Ugh. Does it ever end?

Before I talk myself out of it, I call him.

He picks up on the third ring, his voice out of breath. "Hey. How's your first day in the new office?"

Tension eases out of me once I hear him, and I relax into what is becoming my favorite-ever office chair. "Not bad. Spent the morning with my temporary assistant unpacking and planning. And I have a meeting with some of the board after lunch."

"Nice. Did you get assigned a young male intern who hangs on your every word?"

I laugh. "That would've been funny. Not to mention awkward. No, the woman's name is Tammy. She's an experienced office worker. Has a good head on her shoulders. I like her. What are you up to?"

"Working on the walls in my apartment. It's a dirty job. Drywall dust is everywhere." He sounds happy. Not like the tired man who worked a corporate job late into the night a couple weeks ago.

"Are you dropping hints that you'll need to sleep at my place tonight?" I know he has several empty apartments being renovated, in a pinch he could sleep in any of them, but I like teasing him.

His voice drops to a seductive whisper. "I promise to make it worth your while."

I squirm in my seat, all too aware of what his heated rasp feels like against my skin. "Oh really?" I tease. "I'm not so sure I believe you." A quick glance reveals my office door is shut. "How exactly will you do that?"

"Naughty girl. You want me to tell you?"

"Uh-huh."

"I think I'll start with a shoulder massage..." His voice drops an octave. "And then when you're good and relaxed, I'll roll you over and pin your arms over your head..."

My mouth becomes dry while I picture his scenario. I audibly swallow, eager for him to continue. "Yes...?"

His answering chuckle raises the hairs on my arm. "Well now... you'll just have to wait and see."

I'm giddy when we end the call a few minutes later. Giddy as in you're-acting-like-a-teenager-you-freakin'-idiot. I'm falling for him. Hard. What the hell am I going to do if he doesn't feel the same way?

Chapter Two

Tony

I slip my cell into the back pocket of my work jeans and try to calm my racing thoughts. Cock ring? A tingle of awareness slides over me, settling in the base of my shaft. How would it feel? What prompted her to buy it? One thing that woman's not is boring.

Sure, she looks and sometimes acts like a shy little thing, but when she lets out that inner sex kitten—watch out! A smile curves my lips as I reach down to adjust the growing hard-on in my pants. Would it make me last longer? It's not like I'm a quick shooter, but I'm curious. Would it hurt?

Down, boy!

Jesus, I've got it bad.

I return my attention to the job, determined to push the sexual thoughts from my mind. My only recourse would be to jack-off and I'd rather save my excitement for Heather.

Let's see... where was I? Oh yeah, mudding the drywall tape. This part is so tedious. Best to focus on *why* I'm doing it. I'm doing it for her. It'll be the best photography studio any budding shutter-bug could hope for.

Large windows to the left allow for excellent morning light—perfect for an artist to work in. Once I get paint on the walls and the flooring finished, I'll be able to set up the high-end computer, professional printer, movable backdrop, and lighting equipment.

I can't wait to spring the surprise on Heather. And hey, if it leads to her spending lots of time here then that means it's a job well done.

Now I'll just have to take care of her transportation issue to and from the city. Does she even have a driver's license? So many people living in the city don't even know how to drive. I wonder if she'd like a convertible? My youngest brother Gino owns a BMW dealership in Paramus. I'll have to call him and see what he's got on the lot that might suit her.

I can almost hear my best friend Marcus in my head. Dude, you bought her a car?

Screw it. Maybe I just won't tell him. What's the point of having all this money if I can't do what the hell I want with it? The old anxiety I used to feel over not having enough money tries to rear its ugly head. But I squash it like the useless lie it is. My mom is happy in her small stone cottage in Upper Montclair and Gino is successful on his own.

They don't need me to protect them anymore and I can finally pursue my own dreams. Dreams I hope will include Heather.

What are you waiting for? Just do it, fool.

Impulsively, I pull my phone back out and dial my little brother.

"Aaannn-thooo-Neee!" He drags out my name like we used to as boys growing up in Jersey City. A smile instantly curves my lips. "Great to hear from you," he continues. "What are you up to?"

"Geee-Nooo," I reply in kind. "Shopping for a car. Can you hook me up?"

"Is something wrong with the 750Li you bought last year?"

"Nah, it's good. Just need another car."

"You have four. How many can one guy drive?"

"Technically I don't have four cars. One is a pickup truck for the reno projects and another is an SUV for winter."

"Semantics, Ton. But hey, it's your money. You want another vehicle, I'll hook you up."

"This one isn't really for me."

"Oh? Who's it for? Mom is fine in the car I gave her last year."

I hesitate. What do I call Heather? "Girlfriend" doesn't seem to cover it and "lover" sounds like some crappy line out of a chick flick. "I'm seeing a woman who lives car-less in Manhattan. I'd like her to be able to drive out to my place more easily."

"Your place? Don't you live in those fancy digs Apollo owns near the park?"

Shit. I haven't told my brothers or Mom about my new employment status. Should have thought this out better before I called. *Lust will do that to you, idiot.*

"I... uh... resigned last week. It was time. I needed a change."

"Holy shit! That's some change." A hint of worry enters my brother's tone. "What are you doing now?"

"I'm working on my buildings in Hoboken. Getting new units ready for renters. Hiring contractors, doing some work myself. And before you open your mouth and judge—I'm liking it. A lot."

"Why would I judge you? You've got more money in the bank than anyone I know. It's about time you slow down—enjoy life before you're old and feeble."

I choke on my laughter. "Thanks. Marcus gave me shit and I guess I didn't want to hear more from you."

"Marcus is a pansy pretty-boy. Tell him he can kiss my hard-working ass. Or better yet, I'll tell him myself when we meet up for poker."

"Yeah, hard-working in your air-conditioned luxury car dealership." He knows I'm teasing. I may have lent him the initial money to start the place four years ago, but he paid the funds back within a year.

"Okay, back to the woman. A car is pretty freakin' huge as far as gifts go. Does Mom or Vinnie know? Are you going to introduce her to the family?"

"No, they don't." I side-step his last question. It's too soon for introductions to my two brothers and our mom. "I might just tell her it's an extra of mine and she can use it when she needs to."

"Uh-huh. Because then it won't be such a big deal that you're buying a woman a car? Come on, Tony. Buying a car is more expensive than an engagement ring. You should really let her meet Mom if you're thinking along those lines."

"Hey, I didn't call for relationship advice. Shove it."

"Ah, there's the domineering brother I know and love. All right then, for the car, what were you thinking—sporty or economical?"

"If I was thinking of an economy car would I be calling you?" Before he can shoot off a retort I continue, "Sporty. But she's not a flashy person. No red."

"How about a Z4 or a 640i convertible?"

"Which is better for all weather driving? I want her in something safe."

"They're all safe, idiot. BMW doesn't make shitty cars. But, the 640i will be better in the winter."

We haggle some more about color and features, stressing I'd like a demo model so it has a few thousand miles on it, and then end the call after the details have been hammered out. Gino will have the car delivered to my place by Wednesday. I wonder if I should just give it to her or tell her I'd like her to use it whenever she'd like? I've never given a car to a woman before, I don't know how she'll react.

Whatever. As long as she's happy, I'm happy.

Can life really be as simple as that? Yes—right now I think the answer is a definite *yes*.

I pick up the trowel and start on the third layer of mud on the drywall seams. At this rate, I should be able to apply a primer coat of paint tomorrow. The steady work over the next hour leaves me calm and clear-headed, filled with a different sense of satisfaction I never found at Apollo. It's as if the physical jobs invoke a visceral reaction, a deep-seated need to accomplish a task with results you can see.

Around two I clean up and leave for the city. I grab an overnight bag with a few things for later, hoping to store the items at Heather's, and toss it in the back of my car.

Rather presumptuous to assume you can keep a toothbrush there, isn't it?

He who takes risks, gets laid. Or something like that.

Smile firmly in place over my wittiness, I rev the engine and pull out of the garage, eager to be closer to Heather. Maybe I should surprise her at her house later with dinner? Show her I have some domestic talents as well. But damn, how am I going to get in? I wonder if she'd be willing to give me a key. It would certainly be more convenient, but she might not be ready for that step yet.

I use the voice activated system in my car to send her a text message. "Text Heather Pierce's cell."

The female mechanical voice in my car answers, "Ready for text."

"I'd like to make you dinner tonight at your place, period. Can you arrange for the building manager to let me in, question mark." There was a learning curve associated with speaking the punctuation, but I love the voice activated texting. I think it works better in my car for some reason, too. I never seem to have the same issues with misheard words as when I try to use the voice to text option outside of the car.

The car repeats my message and I tell it to send. I'll check later to see if she responds. A few miles down the road, my cell rings via the car's audio system. Not even bothering to check caller ID on the dash screen, I hit the answer button on the steering wheel.

"Hello?" I try to keep my voice calm instead of sounding too eager with the hope it may be Heather.

"Tony? It's Portia. How are you, honey?"

The smile and good mood slides away. She's the clingy socialite I dated a few weeks. Our fling ended weeks before meeting Heather. "Fine. Why are you calling?"

"Terse and to the point. Just like I remember." She sighs dramatically.

Christ, this woman drives me bonkers. What the hell did I see in her?

Long legs and the ability to suck the chrome off a bumper?

Yeah, that must have been it.

"Look, honey," she says. "We need to talk."

My teeth grind together in frustration. "Isn't that what we're doing?"

"I*n person*, sugar. I have news I need to share."

I'm not falling for some ploy to have her sink her claws back into me. Her parents have a tight leash on her trust fund due to her outrageous spending habits. I got the hell away from her as fast as I could.

"Spill it, Portia. I'm not playing your games."

"No games this time, Tony. *Fine.*" She sighs. "I wanted to do this in person. But you've left me no choice." There's silence on the line, like she's gathering herself. "I-I'm pregnant... and the baby is yours."

My heart pounds in my chest and my knee-jerk reaction almost punches the gas pedal. I swerve onto the shoulder and slam the car into park. "No fucking way. We used protection."

"Darling, didn't you know? Condoms are only effective ninety-seven percent of the time."

Our relationship may not have lasted long, but I thought I knew this woman. Sure, she's a money-hungry harpy—but apparently she also has no morals if she's willing to try a stunt like this. If she slept with me so easily how can I be sure she wasn't so free with her affections to others?

"I'm calling bullshit. There's no way that baby is mine."

"Well then, we'll just have to see. Because I fully intend to sue you for child support. Suck on that, you arrogant bastard."

The phone goes dead in the car speaker and all I hear is the pounding of my heart as my happy world crashes around me.

Chapter Three

Heather

My pulse increases as the elevator ascends. Anticipation over seeing Tony waiting for me in my apartment acts like an aphrodisiac *and* a mild stomach-churner. I'm not sure if I'm going to throw up or kiss him senseless when I see him.

Puking on him would be really uncool.

Yeah, to say the least. I take a deep breath and try to calm down. I can do this. I can act normal when I see him. After all, it was his suggestion. It's not like I asked him to come over and cook for me. I called the building manager after my meeting and asked for a copy of the key to be given to Tony when he stopped by. It felt exciting to call him my boyfriend, but the staff member didn't react to the request or wording either way, just reminded me to stop in and sign for it later.

I had a hard time keeping the smile off my face when I finished, practically skipping to the elevator. We haven't actually talked about him moving in or anything, and he isn't, not really. This is just a way for him to come and go easier while I'm at work. A niggling worry in the back of my mind that we might be moving too fast attempts to break into my happiness, but I quickly stifle it.

I'm going to try my best to "live in the moment," as Katrina said after yoga on Sunday. She smiled when I briefly relayed my current status with Tony, thrilled I'd finally found someone who made me happy. She quickly followed with, "Hey, does he have any good-looking single friends who aren't gay?" Since the only one I'd met so far is Marcus and I had no idea if he was single or straight, I told her I'd find out.

The elevator doors open and I step off, butterflies beating against the walls of my bubbling stomach. We've been together less than a month, do I really have the right to ask about setting his friends up with mine? When is too soon for that kind of thing? I walk down the hall, shaking my head over my insane train of thought—I should probably wait a bit. And I'm sure Carla would be über pissed if I didn't find her a hot friend first. Although, at the rate she goes through men she probably wouldn't notice.

I arrive at my door and take a deep breath, sliding my key in the lock. *Now or never. Go for relaxed and not too eager.*

The door opens and the smells of simmering tomato sauce and garlic reach me. Oh. My. God. He's actually cooking for me. I may become a babbling idiot in ten seconds.

"Hi," I squeeze out past my constricting throat. No guy has *ever* cooked for me. This is beyond epic!

"Hey!" Tony's hearty voice floats to me from deeper in my apartment. "I'm in the kitchen."

I toss my bags and light coat on a chair and stand locked in place, unsure if I should rush in and exclaim over his efforts or act like it doesn't faze me. Before I decide, his large frame fills the entrance between the island counter and wall. A tight dark blue t-shirt spans his chest and a pair of well-worn jeans hugs his hips. His dark hair is slightly mussed and his piercing light brown eyes scan me from head to foot.

My mouth dries, the playful banter I used earlier on the phone deserting me now.

"Well hello, darling." His mouth turns up at the corners, but his eyes look distant, slightly preoccupied. Could he have had issues at Apollo when he went in? His forehead is creased, like he has something on his mind. He visibly relaxes as he leans against the counter. "How was your day?"

Instead of answering I step forward and kiss his delectable lips, determined to chase away my own self-doubts and any lingering shadows I see in him. My tongue ventures forward, shyly tracing the edges of his partially open lips. Strong arms snake around me, crushing me to the broad chest I admired a few seconds ago.

"You smell incredible," he whispers before deepening the kiss, bringing the sweet taste of the tomato sauce with him. Basil, oregano, and onion war with the unmistakable flavor that's all Tony. One warm hand leaves my back to stroke down my hair. I twine my own arms around his neck, running a hand through his hair, holding back the urge to hitch my leg around his waist and grind myself against his hips.

My God, one home cooked meal and I'm a wanton hussy. Strangely, I'm okay with that.

After a long intense minute, where I feel Tony's arousal grow to prod my stomach, he breaks our kiss. A tiny whimper of want escapes me.

He rests his forehead against mine, easing back a few inches. "That was some hello kiss."

"I've never had a man cook for me before." I smile, hoping I don't sound as stupid and lame as I fear. "It... uh... brought out some interesting reactions."

Tony's low chuckle sounds very male and self-assured. "That's an understatement." He winks. "I'll be sure to cook for you more often." He steps back and returns to the kitchen, leaving me bereft of his warmth and affection. "Are you hungry?"

Yeah, I'm hungry to jump his bones. Since when does the guy think about food and the girl think about sex? I follow him in, curious to see what he's made. "I can eat whenever. Smells good. What did you make us?"

He picks up a spoon and stirs what's in the saucepan. "Nothing too fancy, don't be too impressed." He replaces the spoon, puts on the lid, and turns off the flame, his brow furrowing as he looks at the stove. "Just gravy with meat I'll serve over pasta. I'll put the water on to boil in a minute."

"Gravy?" I ask.

He shrugs. "It's an Italian thing. Gravy, red sauce... same thing."

The kitchen is spotless. He not only made the meal, he cleaned up as he cooked. Unreal. Maybe this is what happens when a guy has been a bachelor for a while. They learn to cook *and* clean? I think my panties are becoming wet over his domestic prowess.

Could have been that toe-curling kiss.

I reach for the open bottle of wine sitting on the counter and pour myself a glass, topping off his half-full one as well. "How was your afternoon? Did you go into Apollo?"

Tony stiffens and reaches for his glass. "It was okay." He raises a shoulder and takes a drink, his face revealing nothing. "I'll probably have to go in quite a bit the next month."

Something seems off with him. He was certainly present during that kiss, but now he's not quite himself. Could it be me? Nah, that passion wasn't faked. Maybe something at the office is weighing on him more than he'd like to admit.

I take a big gulp of wine to bolster my courage and decide to act daring. I'll bring him firmly to the here and now with what I plan to do. He loved it that night after we danced in the bar. Boldly, I unbutton my blouse, staring at him the entire time.

The tense look on his face fades and he sets down his wine glass. "Hey now, what are you doing? Fun before food?"

What I hope is a sexy smile curves my lips. "Just a simple stress reliever." I slip my blouse off and step closer, roll the fabric into a ball and offer it to him. "Hold this for me?" He accepts the shirt and moves to place it on the counter nearby. "No, hold onto it." He looks at me, an inquiring expression crossing his face. I place my hands lightly over his and steer the shirt toward his face. "Take a deep breath."

He does as I ask and his eyelids drift lower. "God, that's good. What perfume are you wearing?"

"Does it matter?" I ask softly. His eyebrows raise in question. "When I'm done with you, all you'll know is the scent reminds you of me... this moment... and what I'm going to do to you..." I run a hand down his chest and hook my fingers onto the waistband of his jeans.

"Heather," he reaches one hand to stop me, looking awkward. "Today I—"

"Shh..." I silence him by pressing the fabric toward his face and using my other hand to stroke the hard length behind his fly.

He takes another deep breath as I lower myself to my knees and use two hands to open his pants. I'm turned on just at the idea of doing something so brazen, in my kitchen no less, with all the lights on.

The muscles in his abdomen jump as the button pops open. The silence in the kitchen is broken only by the rasp of the metal zipper descending and Tony's increased breathing. I grasp the material at his hips, yanking down his jeans and underwear to mid thigh. His thick, veined erection springs into view, making my mouth water.

Wrapping one hand around the base, I peer up through my lashes at Tony. My discarded blouse is fisted in one hand near his chest and his eyes burn with desire. He opens his mouth to speak but I silence whatever thoughts were about to escape by taking the silky head into my mouth. Salty pre-come leaks out to coat my tongue, exciting me with the evidence of his arousal.

God, he's stunning. The tight six-pack of his stomach tenses at my touch. My fingers trail over the light smattering of hair and follow the vee of his hip down to his crotch. I slide his length in further as he leans against the counter. It's like he's forcing himself to relax and experience the moment. He's really wired tight tonight. Thankfully, I know just what he needs.

Slowly I pump my fist at the root while tunneling my tongue under his girth, lapping at the engorged tip when I retreat. The musky smell of aroused man fills my nostrils, making me wish I had him plunging inside my pussy rather than my mouth. I've never enjoyed being with a man as much as I do Tony. Gradually I increase my pace, massaging his balls in one hand while my head bobs.

Tony's moans fill the air and he reaches out to cup the back of my neck, tentatively applying pressure to encourage my actions. I've never been able to take a man as large as him all the way back in my throat, but I love the feel of him inside me just the same.

After getting him good and slick, I open my mouth as wide as I can, eager to see how far I can take him. Pressure expands my jaw, igniting a tinge of fear I may start to gag. So far so good. I push harder, hoping to drive his length past the three quarter mark. Tight skin scrapes along my back teeth and I worry I'm hurting him.

"Holy shit, Heather," Tony rasps. "That feels fucking incredible."

I back off a little bit, unable to go any further, and slowly pump his cock in and out, one tight fist still locked at his base. Wetness gathers at my opening, urging me to slip my hand down to pleasure myself. I release his smoothly shaved ball sack and reach under my skirt, shoving aside the scrap of fabric covering my heated mound.

"That's it, baby. Play with your pussy."

I slide off his cock and lick the head like it's my favorite ice cream cone, glancing up to see him watching my every move. My fingers encounter the slippery folds under the silk, delving lower to the wet opening and then spreading the moisture over my clit. I waste no time, rubbing the hard nub furiously while my other hand pumps his cock.

"I want you to come, Tony. And I want to taste every inch of you while you do."

"Will you be able—?"

Before he finishes his question my mouth slides back over his dick, bringing a shudder of pleasure from the big man. The familiar tingle of a hard and fast orgasm builds inside me, ready to crest from my ruthless ministrations.

I quicken my pace, shuttling him in and out of my mouth while my pumping fist races to catch up.

Before I can bring him relief, my own pleasure races to engulf me. My head pauses as the starbursts explode behind my eyes, lighting my entire body with shuddering spasms. I moan around his flesh, unable to focus on my previous rhythm while my peak is upon me.

Tony's own need drives his hips forward. The grip on my head lessens, like he's worried he may shove me onto his length. I open wide, forcing myself back to the task at hand, and start to suck, hollowing my cheeks with the intense suction. The added pressure draws a series of whispered pleas from my lover before warm liquid floods my throat. After the jetting spurts have stopped, I swallow every last drop and lick the tip as I pull away.

I rest my head on his thigh while the two of us recover, waiting for the coordination to return to our muscles.

Firm hands grasp under my arms and lift me. Tony pulls me into a tight embrace. "That was amazing," he whispers, peppering my face with tiny kisses. "What brought that on?"

I shrug, not sure if I should voice the worry that grew inside me at his perceived distance. "You seemed like you needed to relieve some stress."

He sighs, rubbing his five o'clock shadow lightly against my forehead. "I did have a difficult afternoon. And damn... you managed to wipe it all away. Thank you."

"Want to talk about it?"

Resolve settles over his face before he hugs me tight once more. "Nah. I can handle it. I don't want anything to sour our time together." He leans away and kisses me hard. "Besides, we need to eat so I can get you naked and return the favor."

Chapter Four

Tony

The rest of the evening was like every other night I've experienced with Heather by my side—hot, sweaty, and freakin' incredible. We explored each other's body, learning more about what aroused us. She never knew a man humming against her pussy felt so good, and I had to hold back from chuckling as I went through every hard rock tune I could muster—twice.

The look of pure ecstasy on her face... simply priceless. She moaned and writhed, the noises and movements escalating until she was bowing off the bed, and begging me to fuck her. Oh, and man, did I ever. The musky, spicy scent of her perfume filled my head and drove me hard to a big climax. I've never reacted to a woman's perfume before, and now I can't get it out of my mind.

Her shy smile this morning when she woke next to me had me wishing for a camera. What I wouldn't give to capture all these early moments of discovery and bliss for a lifetime of memories to look back on. I wonder if she'd let me take pictures of her? I may not have the skill she has with a camera, but I know beauty when I see it. One shot right after she orgasms would be amazing. I'll have to see if I can talk her into it.

Today I plan to work on her photography studio in my apartment. After yesterday's last sanding, the walls are ready for primer and color. I'm going the untraditional route and plan to paint the walls a pale blue. There will be enough white with the backdrop area and I don't think the whole place needs to look like a sterile slate. The commercial photo printer I ordered should be arriving tomorrow, along with Heather's new car.

How will she react to the convertible? Should I play it off like I planned and say the car was one I don't drive much? Heather is the first girl I've dated, in I don't know how long, who doesn't know my net worth the moment we go out to dinner. It's refreshing.

Since she doesn't know what I'm worth, she might balk at such a pricey gift. Yeah, maybe presenting it like she's borrowing one of my cars would be the smartest option.

Everything feels like it's progressing smoothly... until I think of Portia. My resolve hardens to keep any stain from what we share—yesterday's phone call from Portia being the first thing that comes to mind. There is no way I will let some conniving ex-girlfriend ruin what we've found. If the woman really is pregnant then I'll deal with what to do next. No need to borrow trouble without any actual proof. She could be lying like that Tasha chick I dated five years ago. Another nightmare I'd rather not dwell on too long.

Do these gold-digging bitches all think guys are so dumb that we'd fall for some stupid trap without certified blood work from a lab? Those damn drugstore tests are wrong a lot of times.

I push the mean thoughts away and focus on Heather again. She left for work around seven, despite my blatant enticement she should join me in bed for another round of sex.

Damn, I should have thought of the black leather cock ring. I bet that would have tempted her to leave a little later for work. I'd hate for her to become what I was —a driven workaholic who practically lived at the office. A smile curves my face as I contemplate all the fun ways I'll remind her of what really matters in life.

As I lock up, still in awe she gave me a key to her place, my cell phone rings. Fuck. Portia.

I answer, wariness in my tone, "Yeah?"

"I know our call yesterday didn't go well, but we really need to talk."

I jab the down arrow on the elevator, wishing I was anywhere but here for this phone call. "Okay, what do you need to say?"

She sighs. "I'd rather speak face to face. Discuss things like rational adults."

My anger at her conniving ways bubbles to the surface. "Yeah, I bet you would. If you're not actually pregnant you'd try and lure me into bed so the pregnancy would be a reality after the fact. No thanks. Not going to happen. What do your parents think of this latest scheme of yours?"

She affects a hurt tone. "It's not a scheme, Tony. I really am pregnant. I haven't told them yet. But they always liked you."

"Uh-huh, sure. I met them briefly at a charity function we all attended. We spoke for possibly three minutes, tops. It's not like you took me home for Sunday dinner."

She sniffs loudly, possibly real emotion, possibly staged for my reaction. "Still. They remember you."

Remember my money more likely. They acted like they were thrilled she was finally dating a man they approved of. Yeah, more like someone else qualified to pay for their spoiled daughter's expensive habits. "How far along are you?" The elevator arrives and I enter, then select the lobby level.

"Seven weeks."

I do the quick math in my head. I was with her one last time a few weeks before I met Heather. It could match.

Remembering what I went through with Tasha I say, "Are you sure, or are you just guessing? Have you been to a doctor yet?"

"It was a home test. My first doctor visit is scheduled for tomorrow." She hesitates. "I was hoping you might want to come with me."

The doors open and I step out, the brightness of the spring morning flooding the lobby with light. God, this can't be happening. Not now, not when I have finally found happiness with someone. "In case you can't tell, I'm not thrilled with this development, Portia. I have no desire to go to the doctor's with you." I have a hard time holding back the vehemence in my voice. "Let me know when you have blood work from a real lab saying you're pregnant. Then we'll go from there."

I hear a small sob escape her as I step into the sunshine and start down the sidewalk. "You don't have to be such a bastard. We were really good together."

I abruptly stop in place, the sea of morning commuters parting and walking around me. "Are you fucking kidding me? We dated for two weeks. That's not 'together.' That's a couple of dinners, a charity event, lots of sex, a weekend in Vegas, and me buying you whatever your heart desired—which if I recall was quite a bit."

"But I wanted more."

Could that be the heart of what this is about? She wanted more of me, wanted us to be together so she made up this whole pregnancy thing? Or was she really after more money the whole time we dated?

"Yeah, well, I didn't. You turned out to be just another spoiled rich girl more concerned with parties, clothes, diamonds, and weekend getaways. There's no way in hell that's what I want for the rest of my life."

I hang up, thoroughly shaken that Portia rattled me this badly.

Now I don't want to drive out to Hoboken yet. I need to clear my head before working on something that matters to me. Maybe I'll stop by Apollo and corral Marcus into getting a coffee. Someone's got to have tried this crap on him before, right?

"Sure I remember Portia. Isn't she the loud chick you were banging in the back bedroom on the jet that time we flew to Vegas?"

"No, that was Tara."

Marcus smiles. "Oh, yeah. She was freakin' hot."

I shake my head in disgust. Jesus, I really was a man whore. What the hell would Heather think of all the women? Is she the jealous type or the live-and-let-live type? I run a hand over my forehead, massaging away the knot of tension forming between my temples. I could screw up this relationship before it ever gets off the ground.

"So which one was Portia again?" Marcus asks.

"Maybe you never met her. She was my date at the Children's Hospital fundraiser, the one Nikko donated a bunch of money to. Short reddish-brown hair. Nice rack. Long legs. Late twenties. Loves to party. Her parents are wealthy, but she's got a habit of plowing through her trust fund allocation each month like money grows on trees."

My best friend nods. "I recall the accounting paperwork for that event." Marcus heads the financial department for Apollo Industries, the large conglomerate where I used to acquire smaller companies. "But I didn't go. I'd remember someone like that—in an 'avoid them like the plague' way. Do you think she's telling the truth?"

"Damned if I know. I'll just have to wait and see. Have you ever had a situation like this happen to you?"

A look of compassion crosses his face. "No, man. I don't rank high enough on the wealthy social scale to attract the kind of... uh... materialist women you have." He tries a joke to lighten the mood. "Although it's been great being your wing man and getting their less-vacuous friends for a hook up."

I grunt and stare at my coffee. I never minded dating the party girls who were after my money because I knew they were temporary. In and out of my life quickly. Never someone I'd take home to meet my mom or worry about long term.

"Are you going to tell Heather?"

"Hell no. Wouldn't that be the kiss of death in a new relationship? What the hell would I say, 'Hey, I may have gotten this vapid, money-hungry socialite pregnant. But don't worry, she means nothing to me. It was just mindless sex and a spending spree.'"

Marcus smiles weakly, clearly feeling my pain. "Yeah, I bet that would go over like a fart in church."

I smile at the old phrase my mom used to say. My sweet Catholic mother who would kill me if she found out I got a girl pregnant and didn't intend to marry her. "I am so screwed."

"Not necessarily. Could Portia have been with someone else around the same time you were dating her? Maybe you're not the dad?"

I stifle an involuntary gag over the term "dad." I thought someday, maybe in the far distant future, it might happen, but never like this. I grab onto Marcus's suggestion with a bright burgeoning spike of hope in my chest. "Well, she did like to party. You're right. If she is pregnant it might not be mine."

Marcus claps a hand on my shoulder as he rises from the bistro table. "Hold onto that thought, man. It might work out in the end." He tosses his paper cup into a nearby garbage container. "I've got to get back to work. Are you coming by the office later this afternoon to help transition more accounts over to Brian?"

I scowl at the mention of the annoying man and shake my head no. "Might as well go up now since I'm here." I glance down at my jeans, uncaring I won't be dressed appropriately. "It's kind of nice not having to wear that monkey suit anymore."

Marcus fake shudders and turns away. "Heathen. Next you'll be burning your silk neck ties on that rooftop slum you own in Jersey."

I shove him in the back while we cross the lobby. "Shut up, pretty boy. I'd invite you out to see my 'slum,' but you might mess up your precious metrosexual manicure on the commute."

My old college friend buffs his nails on his suit lapel. "Wouldn't want that, would we? I've got an image to uphold."

"Loser."

"Sperm donor."

A sharp bark of laughter rips from me as we enter the elevator. "Low blow, man."

"That's what she said."

After lunch I'm more than ready to see the last of Apollo for a while. I grab a cab to the parking garage housing my car and drive out to Hoboken. I think I'll stay there tonight so I can push through and get the painting done before the printer and studio supplies get delivered. That way I can set up everything and surprise Heather by Friday.

Feeling good for the first time since Heather left for work this morning, I'm looking forward to the rest of the day. Maybe with enough positive thinking, Portia won't really be pregnant. Or if she is, the baby won't be mine. God, a man can hope.

Chapter Five

Heather

It's Wednesday morning, a little past eleven, and my head is already pounding. I swear, if I have to go through much more "settling in" paperwork, I'm going to scream. And not in a good way like I did Monday night with Tony.

My face heats thinking about it, the memory of his thrusting hips drives some of the headache away, too. Much to my dismay, we didn't get together last night. He was working on his place 'til late and had to crash there due to deliveries he's expecting early today.

I hate to admit it, but I'm really getting used to having him by my side while I sleep. It's not like I tossed and turned last night or anything, but suffice it to say my big bed was quite cold without his solid bulk to warm it.

My fingers itch with the urge to text him and see how his day is going, but I refrain. Texting my boyfriend while

I'm supposed to be helping solve the company's cash flow issue isn't the most productive way of spending my time.

I push aside the latest mound of HR forms to clear my desk blotter. The meeting with the sales team starts soon and I need to brush up one more time on what I'll be expected to cover. My creative financial gymnastics last week may have saved the company from a hostile take-over, but if we don't increase revenue soon we'll be screwed.

Oliver mentioned hiring a batch of new sales people. With luck, it does the trick and my new dream job isn't short lived. As I immerse myself in the figures, a calm steals over me at the familiar task. Numbers never lie. No matter how an executive might try and spin doctor results, the black and red of accounting is pretty damn clear.

In thirty minutes, Tammy knocks on my door. "Heather?"

I glance up, a pen clamped between my teeth. "Uh-huh?"

"The meeting starts in five. Thought you might want to head over to the conference room."

"Thanks." I smile my gratitude. "Time got away from me for a moment."

She bobs her chin and returns to her desk. I gather up my tablet to take notes and grab a few files in case I need to reference numbers specifically.

Oliver, Paul, and Carlos, our dynamic head of sales, are already seated. There are several more people, most

I've never seen before, milling near the food laid out in the back on a long credenza.

I slide the files out of my arms and lower myself into a chair near Oliver. He glances up briefly and nods a greeting. While the food is mobbed, I access the notes app on my tablet, and then double-check everything. The overall revenue numbers aren't strong. Nor is the company's outlook if we can't generate a few real prospects quickly. Here's to hoping Carlos instills some enthusiasm and excitement in the new recruits.

Carlos ushers everyone to their seats, then reads today's agenda aloud. I listen half-heartedly, my mind drifting to the statistics I'll be asked to explain.

"Before we go further," the Latino in his late forties says, "I'd like to take a moment to personally introduce the new additions to our sales team." He gestures individually to each person seated at the other end of the long table, saying their name and where they worked previously. I take the time to make eye contact with each one and offer a welcoming smile.

My heart seizes in my chest as my gaze lands on the fifth person, a self-confident smirk plastered on the familiar face.

"And Jimmy Davenport, who formerly worked as the star salesman for United Planet Advertising." Carlos's voice rises with exuberance, but all I hear is the screaming in my head. "He was a tough one to sway into joining Parkerson, and I'm glad he's here." Looking like he realizes his last comments may have sounded like favoritism he quickly amends, "As I am to have all of you joining us."

It can't be. But my eyes don't lie. The ex-boyfriend who made me feel like a doormat and crushed my self-esteem is a mere fifteen feet away. Looking smug and good-looking as hell. The bastard. Couldn't he have gained like forty pounds and become slovenly after we broke up? Would have fit his true personality much better than the slick facade he presents to the world.

One of the new guys sitting next to Jimmy slaps him on the shoulder in a show of friendly competition. "Sure, start show-boating before the first deal closes. That would be right up your alley, Jimmy."

The corner of my ex's full mouth curves in a calculated aww-shucks grin. A dimple appears in one tanned cheek and a twinkle lights his dark blue eyes. Always a master of timing, he wisely refrains from speaking while looking around the table at his new co-workers, a friendly "I'm harmless" expression on his face.

I know how his mind works. It wouldn't do to come across as pompous and arrogant right out of the gate. He'll save that for later, after they all feel open to him. Goddammit! I can't freakin' believe I've got everything I want in my life, more than I ever dreamed of, and he has to come waltzing back in.

There's no surprise in his eyes when his attention finally lands on me. He knew where I worked eighteen months ago when we dated, and it sure as hell wouldn't be that hard to find out I'm still here. Hell, he probably asked Carlos in his interview.

The rest of the meeting continues in a fog as I try to process the situation. Why is he here? With his professional reputation he could work anywhere he wanted. No need to be at Parkerson unless he wanted to be.

At the end, I focus on gathering my things, amazed I was able to coherently go over my data when called upon. The urge to rush out of the room and hide in my office overwhelms me, but I rein it in. I can't show weakness when dealing with Jimmy. He'll use it and make my life a living hell.

The skin on my arm tingles as the waft of expensive cologne tickles my nose. "Hey, stranger. Fancy seeing you here." He opens his arms for a hug and wraps them around me in a quick, courteous embrace. My arms are folded over my belongings and pinned to my chest. I make no move to return the physical greeting.

"Yeah, hello to you, too," I say in a level tone. "You knew I worked here. What did you expect?"

He steps back and shrugs one shoulder. "It's been awhile. I hoped I'd run into you eventually." His eyes linger on my hair, he always loved to fist its length while force-feeding me his cock or pinning me to the bed while he grunted over my passive form. God, I hate who he drove me to become. "But never expected to see you on the board." A warm smile curves his mouth. "You're looking good. *Real good*. Life has been treating you well."

His intensity is laser sharp, like he's looking into my soul. I always loved and hated that. It was as if he knew things about me I never did.

Flustered, I remain silent, looking for a way to escape without appearing outright rude.

"Congrats on the new position. It's about time they noticed what a treasure they have in you." My eyes dart away, unable to hold his penetrating stare any longer. His voice softens as if he senses my uneasiness. "Lord knows I never did until you were gone."

Carlos steps through the conference room door from the hall. "Jimmy," he calls. "Let's get you set up with the others in the sales department."

"Yes, sir." His eyes travel up and down my body, desire heating in their depths. "See you around, Heather."

I nod, my head moving in a jerky fashion. My insides quiver with a mix of fear and confusion. He forced me into a dark spiral of low self-esteem—cheated on me, claiming I was awful in bed—why the hell is he being so nice now? And what the hell am I going to do about him working here?

Tony reaches across the table to clasp my hand. We're at a Chinese restaurant near my place, waiting on the check. "Earth to Heather. You've been miles away for the past ten minutes. What's on your mind?"

I've been lost in my thoughts most of the evening, unsure what to say about Jimmy working for my company. All my old insecurities churned up, making me feel raw and exposed for the rest of the day. I don't want secrets between us, so I might as well bite the bullet.

A sigh escapes as I gently squeeze his fingers, glad for his reassuring touch. "The board was introduced to the new sales staff today."

Tony nods his head, "Yeah, and? Hopefully they will line up new clients for Parkerson soon."

"That's the goal." What little food I ate bubbles in my stomach, threatening to evacuate. "One of the new sales guys is an ex-boyfriend." I stare at the table, afraid to look in his eyes where he can see my fear. "It ended over a year ago. He was kinda an asshole."

"Asshole?" Tony's tone changes and he tugs my fingers to get my attention. "That's a strong descriptor coming from you. Is it that guy I met at the restaurant?"

I shake my head, refusing to look up, ashamed there are tears forming in my eyes. "No, that was Rick. We didn't date all that long. This is Jimmy. We dated about six months..." My voice trails off. I'm unsure how much to tell him. God, I feel so stupid. Why did I bring this up?

"Hey." He leans toward the table, ducking to meet my eyes. When that doesn't work he puts a finger under my chin and tilts my face up to his. "What happened, honey? This isn't like you. Why the tears?"

The compassion on his face undoes me, and the tears spill down my cheeks. "He liked to put me down. Made me feel like dirt. Told me that I was lucky to have him. Cheated on me. Was an insatiable womanizer with anything in a skirt." Surprise lights his eyes and I rush on. "I realize now the situation was partly my own fault. I allowed it to get as bad as it did."

I take a shaky breath and swipe a napkin under my eyes. "God, I feel so stupid saying this out loud. It really was nothing—or at least it feels like nothing now. He was nothing. I've grown into a different person and see how my actions and participation in his slow destruction of my self-esteem was toxic. It all happened so gradually I didn't realize what was happening until it was too late."

When I finally feel strong enough to meet what I can only assume will be disapproval in his gaze, I'm taken aback. A dark intensity crosses Tony's face. A look I've never seen on my handsome lover. He looks angry. And determined. Almost furious enough to punch something.

"He's a predator. I know exactly the type of guy you're describing. The only way they can keep a woman is to break her down so she'll never leave him. At the same time, they go after more conquests, never satisfied or happy."

I'd never thought of Jimmy that way. With his suave manners and polished good looks, I was out of my element, pleased a man like that wanted to be with me. If it hadn't been for Carla's steady friendship, I might not have permanently ended things when I caught him cheating. She gave me the courage, and she stood by me while I cried my eyes out for months.

"What are you going to do? Please tell me I can pound his face into the sidewalk. God, that would feel so good."

I laugh, strangely pleased with Tony's immediate offer to avenge me and keep me safe. Resolve settles inside me. "Thanks. Just talking about it has made me feel tons better. I'll handle this creep. I've got a new job and there's a new me." I smile, glad the tears have left. Tony looks a little disappointed I didn't take up his gallant offer to beat up an old boyfriend like we were in junior high. "But I promise if things get out of hand I'll let you know."

Chapter Six

Tony

The gleam off the BMW's shiny surface causes me to squint. Heather's new car arrived two days ago before we met for Chinese, but she has no idea—which is exactly how I want it. After all, it's not a surprise if I tell her. And I'm still unsure how I'm going to spring it on her. Maybe I'll wait and see if an opportunity presents itself.

Nah... that's almost like taking the coward's way out. Perhaps I should do a big surprise reveal. Maybe one of those big bows used in car commercials. No, if she thinks it's a gift she'll probably refuse. Best to stick with my original plan and tell her it's a car I'm not driving much and would like her to use so she can come out to Hoboken easier.

She's deep in my thoughts. No matter what I do it's like all roads lead back to Heather. Last night I stayed at her place after dinner. No matter how I phrased it, she was unwilling to let me help with this ex-boyfriend situation at work.

Considering my own duplicity with not telling her about the fiasco with Portia, I wisely backed off to let her handle it on her own, even if doing so went against every male instinct I possess. I remember when my mom became involved with a loser like Heather's ex after my dad died. In a matter of a few months, she'd shrunk into herself, becoming a shadow of the loving woman who held the family together during all the tough years of my dad's excessive drinking and gambling.

At the time she dated this guy, I was working a crappy day job while going to college at night. One rare day off from work and school, I really saw who my mom had become. That night my brothers and I sat her down for a long talk.

We gave her an ultimatum: either the new guy went away on his own or we'd make him go. Even though I'd never been in a real fist fight, just the normal violent skirmishes three brothers will engage in, I was good sized. I knew my brothers and I could protect my mother if the man became physical—which is where it was going based on the shit he screamed at her when he thought her sons weren't around.

It was a dangerous situation, one I'm glad she emerged from safely, and it makes me doubly glad Heather got out from under her ex, too.

I know I haven't treated all my casual flings as they may have wanted—with an engagement ring and promises of undying love—but I never treated them poorly or tried to destroy their self-esteem, either. Cheating on them never came into play because nothing lasted longer than a month.

Wanting to shake off the dark memories, I admire the new car, running a hand along a sun-warmed section of the hood. In a moment, I remember the deliveries waiting upstairs. I click a button on the key fob to engage the car locks and man the alarm, then return to my apartment on the fifth floor. All the photography equipment I ordered arrived yesterday. I spent the day arranging things and testing the lighting.

Between the backdrop, computer equipment, professional printer, lighting poles, umbrella thingies and all the other numerous gadgets a proper studio should have, I think I've created a great space for Heather's hobby. I grab a long-stemmed lighter from the grilling drawer in my kitchen and return to the studio to light the wicks on the four vanilla candles placed around the room.

The guy at the paint store recommended the candles for neutralizing the last of the odor from the low VOC paint. With luck, the fumes will be gone in a couple of hours.

Afternoon light streams through the large windows, the building's southern exposure making this a perfect choice for daytime work. I grab a remote off a nearby table and press a button. Hidden shades unroll, filtering the strongest light and granting the room privacy from anyone looking in. There's also a light blocking option if Heather decides she needs no outside light.

As the last of the fabric drops into place, a lone sunbeam glints off the metal chains draped over a stool centered on the backdrop. My cock stirs in anticipation. I can hardly wait to spring this room on Heather. The camera I bought her sits fully charged on a high table just inside the door. She can't miss it when she arrives later. Maybe leaving her notes would help. I can't exactly meet her at the door with what I planned.

My phone rings. I dig it out of my back pocket, hoping it's Heather. I should change the ring tone so I know when she's calling.

Damn, you sound like a besotted sap.

What of it? I don't give a flying fuck if I sound whipped. All I think of is the look on her face when she walks in later.

Dread hits me when I check the screen. Tension tightens my shoulders as I hit the answer option.

"Hi, Portia."

"Hey, lover," she says in a low, throaty voice.

Anger boils under my skin, cold and quick. "Cut the crap. I'm not your lover and I never will be again."

"Not the nicest way to talk to a pregnant woman, you know."

"So you got the blood work back from the doctor? It's official?"

"Yes, I did. And yes, I'm officially pregnant. Don't you think it's time we sat down and had that chat, Tony?

Face to face? I know you say you won't marry me, but we do need to discuss other *important* related facts."

Resentment sits in my stomach like a lead balloon. I was careful when we slept together. The condom never broke. I refuse to believe I'm one of the three percent of unlucky bastards with an "ineffective" condom.

"I'm not just *saying* we won't get married—we won't. It's not going to happen. I don't love you and I refuse to marry anyone out of a sense of obligation. You really think that would benefit a child? And besides, I'm not completely convinced this child is mine. How far along are you?"

"Eight weeks. Why not just call me a whore while you're at it? Don't you think I know who I slept with less than two months ago?"

Picturing the calculating look I often saw in her eye, I have my doubts. She was a party girl through and through. We slept together seven to ten times in the few weeks we were involved—and I by no means lived with her. She easily could have been with someone else.

In my silence, she continues. "The six week mark was the last weekend fling we had in Vegas. Remember the fun we had?" A sigh escapes. "Joining the mile high club on our way out was never so much fun—and comfortable."

Damn, I'm so screwed. What have I done in my life to deserve this? Is someone upstairs looking down and laughing their ass off at me right now? This would be just the kind of shit to make my drunken father laugh until he coughed.

"Whatever, Tony. We need to talk money. Medical bills will begin to mount."

A harsh bark of laughter escapes me. "It always comes back to money with you, doesn't it? Hard to act like an adult when you don't have a job and live off a trust fund. What's wrong, mommy and daddy won't foot the bill?"

"They don't know. I haven't told them."

"Yeah, you should hold off until you know who the father is."

"I do know. It's *you*."

The rage forges into a cold hard length of steel, settled in my spine. "Not until I see a DNA test will I be convinced. I'll call a lab and go for a blood sample. You'll submit to whatever they need to prove that baby is mine or any future conversations we have will go through lawyers." A puff of angry air sounds over the phone. "Do you think I got to where I am by not checking details?"

"No. I think you got to where you are by being a cold, heartless bastard."

I fist one hand in impotent anger and bang it against my thigh. "You change your tune as it suits you. First you want me in your life, then you talk marriage, then you want money. Whatever your game is, Portia, I will not be as easily manipulated as your parents. They've coddled you your whole damn life—and look where you are now; you're leveraging a baby for cash. You're pathetic."

"And when I'm done with you, you'll wish you were described as pathetic. I'll ruin your reputation, I'll take half of your assets, and you know what else? I'll be in your life for the next eighteen years—whether you like it or not. Suck on that, you smug jerk."

The line disconnects and tension spills out of me. Maybe it's time I called a lawyer. I have a feeling this will be getting much worse before it gets better.

After a half a dozen phone calls to lawyers, a private detective, and an appointment to have my blood drawn, I'm feeling much better. The lawyer did advise I try talking to her, to at least attempt to handle things in a civilized manner. Until she's further along we're going to be in a holding pattern for scientific proof. But I've done what I need to do to protect myself and make sure this hormone-filled woman doesn't try and destroy my reputation in the process.

What if it is mine? Have I screwed any chance of a decent relationship with the child's mother? Who am I kidding—Portia would turn around in a flash if enough money was on the table.

With any luck the investigator will pull up enough dirt on her that I'll have my own leverage if she decides to go to the press. I've never really cared for the media attention when I showed up in the social pages, and I couldn't give a rat's ass what the general public thinks of me, but I don't want my family and Heather harassed due to this woman's personal vendetta.

Pushing the afternoon from my mind, I decide to work out. That should help erase the anger and bring my mind under control again. First a run and then lifting weights, followed by a quick shower and then prep for my surprise with Heather. No way in hell am I letting the taint of this situation demolish my chances of happiness with her. She's too important to me.

As I tie my running shoes I refuse to think about what would happen if she found out what was going on. I can't lose her before we even give what we've got a real try.

Chapter Seven

Heather

Anticipation tightens my skin as I shut down my computer for the weekend. Tammy left a little while ago and I could hardly contain the silly grin I wore all day. And who would blame me? Tony texted this morning with instructions a car was picking me up after work at five thirty, and taking me to Hoboken for something special. I have no time to run home and get clothes, so if I wind up staying the night I won't have anything fresh to wear tomorrow.

Like worrying about two-day-old underwear is going to stop me. Hah!

I know he's got something up his sleeve, and mulling on it all day has kept me in a steady state of arousal for hours. Did he snag the cock ring from my nightstand drawer? We never did use it, as just the thought and subsequent conversation left us so busy we never tried it.

A delightful shiver raises the hairs on my arms. God, he's so delectable. And all mine. It really does feel like a dream.

A knock on my door pulls my attention. A tall, lean form rests against the doorframe. Jimmy. Freakin' great.

His intense dark blue eyes pin me to my chair. "What's got you looking like the cat that ate the canary?"

I plaster on a neutral smile, refusing to allow him to see my discomfort in his presence. "Just thinking of the weekend."

"Hmm... any special plans?"

No way in hell am I engaging in anything personal with him. "Not really." I glance pointedly at my watch. It's five fifteen. "Anything I can help you with?"

He saunters into the room, like he has every right to be there. "I'm proud of you, Heather. You really have done well for yourself."

Unsure of how to react to his praise, I nod. He always has an ulterior motive, but I have no idea what his is now. I can't stop the little swelling of happiness in my gut. I will squash any reaction this man pulls from me, and I hate that he's made me feel like I have his approval, when I don't want or need it.

Surely he can't think after catching him in the act, and me realizing what our nightmare of a relationship had become, that we'd ever get back together? But wait, how would he know how I felt if we weren't together any longer? It's not like we spoke after the night I caught him cheating. If Carla had been there when I was throwing his personal items out into the hall she probably would have held me back, preferring to burn everything instead. And it would have felt good.

His attention strays and lingers on the framed photos I took of Tony's building in Hoboken. "I've been thinking about you a lot. I miss what we had." He turns to me and flashes his one thousand watt smile. "There's no one like you."

Unbidden, Carla's snarky voice fills my head. *Oh yeah? Then why did he sleep with those other women and treat you like dirt? Why did he make you cry? Why did he distance you from all your friends and tell you what you could wear? Screw him! Don't let the rat bastard back in your head!*

"Well, that's nice, Jimmy." My voice sounds cold and unfeeling. Good. "But that's the past. I'm not the same person anymore." The doormat who used to take whatever crumbs you offered and patiently waited for more.

His face sobers and a sincere look enters his eyes. "Neither am I."

"Great." I glance away, unable to hold his penetrating stare any longer. "Good for you. Did you stop by for a reason? I need to get out of here."

"Um... yeah, actually. I did." He looks over his shoulder briefly. "Is your assistant Tammy seeing anyone?"

Shock surges to the surface as heat suffuses my face. Oh my God. And here I thought the slimy bastard was interested in me! "I have no idea." Can I really let him make a play for her? I'd never wish him on my worst enemy.

She's a grown woman, it's not like you have any power over her.

"Great." He repeats my earlier response, a sly smile on his face. "Have a good weekend."

Pushing away the apprehension Jimmy's visit left, I settle comfortably in the plush leather of the hired town car. I don't mind the drive to Hoboken, especially when mass transit doesn't come into the equation. It's not that I dislike subways, but they do take longer and aren't always the safest for a woman traveling alone past a certain hour. And buses? Don't get me started. It's like the dying, depressed energy of long-term commuters taints the very fabric covering the bus seats.

A hired car lends an air of luxury to the journey. Nice.

My cell buzzes in my purse, indicating a new text has come in. I fish it out to see Carla's smiling face next to her latest missive.

Katrina, Gemma and I are going out for drinks. Want to join?

Thanks. I text back. *Have plans. Raincheck?*

Loser! ;-) We'll miss you.

Hoping I'll see her later, I ask, *Are you doing yoga this weekend?*

Yes to yoga. C U then! You free for lunch on Monday?

I text back I'm good with lunch on Monday and enter the appointment in my calendar. Call me a nerd, but hey, I'm organized.

A part of me worries about Carla's casual approach to life. Granted, there's nothing wrong with a night out with friends—hell, we all need that every couple weeks, but she's a year older than me. If she doesn't snap out of the college love-'em-and-leave-'em lifestyle, she's going to be single and in her *thirties*. Never a good position for a woman living in Manhattan. It's like the women over thirty-four have this desperate look to them. Afraid of the dwindling child-bearing years left with no husbandly prospects on the horizon.

Geez... Who am I to judge? Maybe Carla is the smart one. I hope she shoots me if I ever feel like I'm desperate to have a guy in my life. Might be time for a future girlfriend pact. No allowing the other to choose a loser simply because we'd be past our prime baby-making years.

Oh, you mean a loser like Jimmy? You really dodged a bullet there. He'd have made sure you were barefoot and pregnant, servicing his "needs" whenever the urge hit him, and when bored, he'd be banging the neighbor. Oh, but hey, only after he made you feel like you were fat and ugly first.

I take a deep breath and push the nasty thoughts from my mind. I will not allow his memory to color my night or my weekend. I'll deal with whatever comes my way regarding him next week.

Leaning back in the seat, I rest my head on the cushion and close my eyes, picturing a tender smile on Tony's face and lingering arousal in his light brown gaze. Heat pools low in my middle as I remember skimming my hands over his washboard abs. I love touching him. His reactions make me feel so... powerful. And desired. What a heady combination.

The car rolls softly to a standstill, not unlike the many throughout the trip at various stoplights, but this time the car shifts into park. I straighten and look out the window to see Tony's building.

"We're here, miss," the driver announces while lifting his gaze in the rearview mirror to meet mine.

'Thank you." I reach for my purse, unsure if I should tip him.

He sees my actions and says, "Don't worry, miss. Everything is already covered, including the tip." Then he turns and hands me a sealed envelope. "This is for you."

I accept it, nod my thanks, and gather my belongings. The driver exits the car and quickly opens my door, a hand held out to assist. Feeling like a movie star, I leave the vehicle, noting a lightness to my heart that wasn't there during the ride.

Tony does this to me. He thinks of what I want or need before I do. He anticipates my desires and fulfills them without request, like I'm a cherished person in his life. As the town car glides into Friday traffic, I open the letter. Inside is a key and a brief note.

*This is the key to my place. The door
code for the main entrance is 1031.
Come on up. I'll be waiting.*

~T

Excitement and something else blossoms in my chest... a yearning. That's what he's made me—eager. I fold the note and place it in my purse. Before turning to the building, a shiny blue convertible parked by the curb catches my eye. *Sweet!* I'm not much of a car person, but I recognize the brand symbol on the hood—BMW. I wonder if this is another one of Tony's cars. He mentioned once that he has a few and the two I've seen are both this make.

That eagerness pulls at me again, drawing me away from the car to race up the steps of the apartment building. I punch in the door code and enter the foyer, glad I'm alone while waiting for the elevator. Within minutes I'm jiggling my new key into the lock, my every nerve on high alert over Tony giving me a key to his place.

This is so huge! Do I make a big deal out of it or let it slide, pretending to be more collected than I really am? I open the door to low playing rock music, and the faint scent of vanilla overlaying construction smells like drywall and paint. Tony's been a busy man. The small foyer contains a table with flowers and another note with my name on it.

Oh my God! How can I possibly stay calm and cool when he's being so freakin' incredible? Who does this kind of stuff for a woman? It's like he's trying to make me fall in love with him. Whoa now. Don't assume. We all know where that leads.

I grab the note, unable to contain my enthusiasm as I rip open the paper. The smile on my face is stretched so tight I'm sure I look like the grinning Joker—slightly crazed with a hint of humor.

> *Leave your work things and come*
> *find me.*

HolyCowHolyCow.... What do I do? Does that mean take off my work clothes, too? Maybe he just means leave my stuff like my coat, bag, and purse? I nod my head, talking to myself in my desperation, "Yeah, that's probably what he means."

I toss my crap on the floor, uncaring where it lands, motivated to find him. I step away and halt. If I leave my stuff like that and he sees it later I will be so busted as a freaked out woman who couldn't hold her shit together. Wanting to kick myself, I pick up my coat and place the other items casually against the wall.

A quick glance reveals a coat hook near the door. Gee, that's pretty obvious. I hang the garment and waste no more time, venturing deeper into the apartment. The kitchen lighting is turned down low, and candles are lit throughout the open floor plan. Warm vanilla wraps around me, relaxing muscles I didn't know were tense. The island is set with plates and cold appetizers under a glass cover.

But there's no Tony. Immediately I turn to the bedroom, striding across the neat living room with quick steps. It would be so like him to be naked and waiting for me on the bed already. Perhaps he set up the food as an after-meal, and the main course is us getting busy.

I giggle in anticipation, heat and desire igniting all my senses. More candles are lit here, but the big bed is made and there's no hot guy waiting for me. What the hell? I look out the large windows to Tony's private roof garden, but see no one out there either. Okay, I'm stumped. The rest of the place is still unfinished, so where else could he be?

Curiosity battles with arousal as I journey down a side hall, looking for my hiding boyfriend. I throw open the first door and freeze in place, shock igniting every nerve ending I possess.

Somehow, someway, Tony created a photography studio—*for me*—in under a week. Pale blue walls glow softly in the filtered light. To my left there's an entire station of computer equipment and several large printers. In the center of the room and to the right, sit various set supplies—light poles, a chaise, stools, fabric rolls, lighting umbrellas, props—and *holyfuckinghell...* there stands my heart's desire—Tony.

Shirtless, his muscled chest glistening like it's been oiled, ripped jeans slung low on his hips, and a devilish smile on his face. Dark messy hair, slightly longer than when we met almost a month ago, curls over his forehead and down his neck. His arms are stretched high, with a metal chain looped around his wrist and secured to a hook in the ceiling. Another shiny chain lies draped over his olive skin, lying across his shoulders to dangle over his chest.

There's a defined ridge behind the fly of his faded jeans, leaving no doubt he's definitely turned on by this scenario he's staged.

"Come on in, darlin'. Grab the camera off the table and let's have some fun."

Chapter Eight

Tony

"Oh my God. You really did this. I'm not dreaming? You're really standing here," Heather's eye sweep me from head to toe, lingering on my crotch, "half-naked and ready for me to take pictures of you."

Her eyes meet mine and I smile slowly. "I'm not adverse to being completely nude, eventually. But maybe without the camera."

Heather's dressed in a dark grey skirt I haven't seen before. It rests just above her knees. She's wearing a bright red blouse and her long black hair spills over her shoulder in a tumble of curls.

She steps deeper into the room, grabbing the camera off a side table in passing. Her red spiked heels, the ones I gave her with the silver heel, rap against the bamboo flooring, their sound ratcheting up my heart rate with every step. Displaying myself like this has had me hard since the driver called to report their projected arrival time. Is she as turned on as I am or did I go too far?

I've never felt such a consuming desire to experiment sexually like I do with Heather. Something about how right we feel together has pushed me beyond my comfort zones. Makes me want to submit and let her lead, just as much as I want to dominate and stake my claim.

Her gaze lingers on my chest and abs, and I can't help it, I flex, hoping to hold her attention longer.

Heather's voice comes out low and sexy. "You look incredible." She raises the camera and starts shooting. "The diffused light playing on your skin—makes you look warm... and utterly lickable."

My hardened length twitches in my pants. The memory of her pink tongue teasing me when I cooked her dinner, and then her painted lips eventually surrounding my cock, leave me shaking, despite the warmth in the room.

"Tilt your head down, angle your chin toward the door." I do as she requests. "That's it. The shadows across your face lend a hint a mystery."

She takes a few more shots, seemingly as spellbound as I am.

"Holy hell," she mutters while aiming the camera. "This is so freakin' hot." The digital rendition of a camera snap fills the silence when she's not speaking. "You do realize you could model for real, right?" She moves the camera from her face for an instant. "And I'm not saying that because I plan on sleeping with you later."

I chuckle softly, stretching into the chains, loving how she makes me feel. Desirable beyond reason—it's empowering. "Yeah, your opinion is completely unbiased."

I'd never really thought about using my physical sexuality to snare a women's attention, but it makes sense such a tactic would work on them as much as it does on us. I tighten my stomach, enjoying the tense and release along my skin. It's going to feel freakin' unreal when we're done to finally slide into her tight sheath. My hips pulse forward once, the fantasy of taking her hard and loud overcoming me.

"Your muscles. They look so... solid. So primed for action. Did you do something or are you always this sculpted?"

"I worked out with weights for an hour before you got here." She's circling me, taking pictures from every angle. "Knew it would make the definition sharper."

A light touch skims over my back. "Holy hell, Batman. Did it ever." She plasters her front to my back, the slide of her silky blouse a whisper of sensation across my skin. The lure of her perfume has me drawing in a deep breath. Only a whiff has me thinking about her sucking me off. Man, I don't think I'll ever get that scent out of my brain—and I don't want to.

Warm lips settle between my neck and shoulder, above the chain. "You, my dear man, are a god."

I laugh, her outrageous words boosting my ego way higher than it needs. "If you say so."

She nibbles my neck slightly, her chin nudging the warmed metal lying over my shoulder. "Oh, I do." One hand snakes around to my chest, then slides down, over my stomach, to cup me through my jeans. "And I can hardly wait until these come off."

My hips thrust forward again, seeking more pressure from her tiny hand. Rucked up like this via the hook I installed has ensured I've been close to the edge since the chains touched my skin.

Is this what obsession is? When you do things you wouldn't dream of, all in the hopes of gaining someone's touch? Of holding their attention long enough for you both to fall into each other's arms and lose your senses in the moment? Or is it thinking about them all the time, unable to get their smile and scent out of your head?

I'm not sure, having never felt it before—but I know I like it. It's exciting and nerve-wracking all at once.

She strokes me through the jeans, then pats my cock and leaves it, almost reluctantly. "Do your arms hurt, raised like that?"

A stiffness creeps in the moment she calls the position to my attention. "Well, they didn't at first." I grasp the chain and pull, raising my feet off the ground, then drop back down. Blood rushes through the elevated limbs, tingling. "I'm good for a little while longer. As long as I keep the muscles moving it's not too bad."

Determination wars with desire on her delicate face. "Good. I'd like a few more this way before I move you."

I suppress a smile. I know exactly how I'd like her to move me. Or at least part of me. A long, stiff part I'd like to see disappear into her flesh. Over and over again.

Long minutes pass, the sexual tension thick enough to choke a horse. At one point she unbuttoned my jeans and lowered the zipper a fraction of an inch. I almost regret wearing anything underneath. It's going to be intense watching her reveal my arousal slowly.

Heather sets the camera down and steps close, pressing her perky breasts against my chest while she reaches above my head.

"Here, let me help get the chain off your wrists." She unnecessarily assists, which I'm sure is a ploy to touch me, although I'm not complaining. She frees one hand, then the other, wiggling against me the whole time. My arms come down and naturally wrap around her waist to draw her closer.

"You're irresistible when you're so... focused." I lean in and kiss her gently on the lips. "Having fun?"

"Yes!" She squees in delight and squirms out of my hold. "I've thought about taking pictures of you—I mean, how could I not? You're so freakin' good looking and well built. But I was worried you'd say no or it might sound... creepy." She trails off as if just realizing what she's revealed.

"So, I'm good looking, huh?"

She swats me playfully and spins away to grab the massage oil I set on a nearby table. "Puh-lease! You know you're good looking. All those woman falling all over themselves for years? You can't tell me you didn't notice."

Her words tighten something in my gut. Yeah, women who wanted me for my money. I push the thought down deep, refusing to focus on it or the reminder of Portia it stirs up.

Tell her! Tell her now, you fool!

No. I ignore the mad chatter in my head. I don't want to taint this moment. And this sure as shit is not the right moment. Perhaps after I make her come three times and she's thoroughly relaxed would be a good time. Plan in hand, I let go of the tension, relaxing once more.

Oil drips onto her palm and she approaches me with a playful glint in her eye. "Oh, you knew, all right." One hand reaches out and smoothes the slippery liquid across my pecs. "But somehow you resisted. Saved yourself for me." She spreads the oil lower, over my abdomen, lingering a little longer than necessary, obviously enjoying the oiling up process. Two clever fingers venture upward to tweak a hardened nipple. "So smart."

Her lips tilt up at the end, and then something crosses over her face. A deep thought, perhaps inner hesitation—I'm not sure what—but her twist on my skin turns painful, drawing a sharp breath from me.

"A part of you likes that, don't you? You like it a little rough." I don't say anything, just stare into her dark brown eyes. "Or maybe what you really like is not knowing what I'll do next and the power you've given me over your pleasure."

She releases the tender flesh and air hisses out of my lungs. "I like taking turns with who's in charge," I say.

Her tongue slides out to moisten her lips. "Is that so bad? You seem to like it, too."

Heather's expression fills with lust. She unbuttons her blouse, stopping midway to reveal skin stained with the blush of arousal. "I do like it. It's powerful... heady... not to mention sexy as hell when you call me 'ma'am.'"

My cock lurches. I *love* calling her ma'am. It's innocent but naughty at the same time—just like she is. "Glad to hear it, *ma'am*." I smile, a fresh idea coming to me. "Would you like it if I wore a cowboy hat while I said it?"

Her gaze becomes unfocused for a moment and she shudders slightly. "Only if you wear a pair of leather chaps, too."

As I picture her words, an image leaps to mind of my erection jutting between a bracket of black leather while I bend her over and take her hard from behind. "I think that can be arranged." I wonder where I can buy leather chaps. I'll be searching the Internet later if that's what she wants to see me in. Have to admit, the idea does sound intriguing. They must make chaps for women, too. Now there's an image I can get behind. Repeatedly. In several positions. Maybe I'll look into buying a crop, as well.

She slips off her blouse, unhooks her bra and lets it slide to the floor, then steps behind me. Her incredibly sexy shoes bring her closer to my height. She molds her heated skin to my back and reaches around to clasp the doubled chain dangling over my chest. "Kiss me," she says while leaning over my shoulder.

I turn my head, meeting her insistent mouth with my own. She tugs on the chain, intensifying the mild sensation of being owned. Right now, if she asked me to lick her pussy for an hour and held me by these metal chains I wouldn't bat an eye or complain once. I'd lavish her sweet flesh with attention until she begged me to stop.

She breaks the kiss, her breath warming my flesh in short pants. "I want you on the chaise. With your pants open. Can you handle that?"

I suppress a smile, excited for her to see my next surprise. "Yes, ma'am."

"Leave the chains on. And don't take off the jeans yet —I want the camera to have only a glimpse of what's beneath."

I do as she bids, unzipping my fly fully and leaning back on the low cushioned lounger. I rest one arm under my head on the armrest to stare at the slim woman behind the lens. She's topless and uncaring, her erect nipples pointing directly at me. The urge to free my cock and stroke it is strong. Sliding my fist up and down the hard flesh while she watches would be intense. Like our first date in her apartment—our intimate picnic in her living room. My hand rubs once over the thin fabric and moves away. Resisting temptation proves difficult.

The camera clicks and she hesitates. "Is that the underwear I bought with the ping pong paddle? I don't remember giving them to you." She emerges from behind the plastic casing, a look of longing and hunger on her face.

"You mean the ones you bought the day you spanked me in my office? Yes. I found them in the bag later. Do you like them?"

She swallows, her throat working with a slight undulation of skin. "Wow. I totally want to kiss your cock through those underwear." Eager eyes devour me with desire and inquiry.

"Like I'd say no to that? It's your shoot." I reach down and cup my erection, rubbing it while I hold her gaze. "You can do whatever you'd like—take whatever you want."

"That's the best offer I've had in years. Be prepared. You've unleashed a succubus." She rests the camera on a nearby stool before unzipping her skirt and letting it fall to the floor. Desire softens her face while heat dances in her eyes. "I want you to lean back comfortably so I can straddle your face easier."

Excitement bubbles inside, but I don't react, just do as she says and ease my arm out from under my neck. I scoot lower and rest my head against the rolled arm, watching her approach. She saunters toward me, a jaunty sway to her hips. Nude thigh high stockings encase her long toned legs, and a red triangle of satin hides the juncture between. She stops near my head and elegantly lifts one leg high, resting the pointy heel on the rolled arm rest close to the low back of the chaise, effectively aiming her pussy right at my mouth.

Firm fingers slide through my hair, fisting near the scalp to sting slightly. "Lick me." Her breathing hitches, sounding like she's gasping for air. "Lick me hard and fast. I want to come all over your face."

A groan of delight escapes me as I pull the thin piece of cloth away from her flesh. "Yes, ma'am."

The musk of her arousal coats the air. My tongue laps one long stroke from her opening up to her clit, savoring the taste. Once I reach the tiny nub her hips begin to circle, grinding against my mouth. I try and focus lower, to drive my tongue deep inside, but she's having none of it. She secures my head in place with a hunk of hair to silently let me know *exactly* where she wants my tongue.

"Oh... yeah... that's it. Holy crap... it's gonna be a big one."

Her body tenses as I increase my ministrations, sucking madly on her tiny clit.

"Oh...." She circles faster, riding my face and taking her pleasure. It's breathtaking to behold.

The leg on the floor starts to shake as she fists a second hand in my hair. "Yes!" She throws her head back and screams her release to the room. I grip her ass, holding her firmly in place while her pleasure overcomes her. Mid-way through I start to hum, determined to drive her higher and draw out her orgasm.

"Oh God! Yes!" No longer circling, her hips thrust back and forth, forcing her pussy up and down on my mouth. If I'm not misreading her bucking body and short shouts, her pleasure spikes again, sending her leaping off the abyss toward another release.

She writhes like a mad woman before drooping, her weight shifting to collapse on the low chaise back. The strength drains out of her and she sighs. She gradually loosens her death grip in my hair, smoothing out the crazy tufts, petting me like one would a jittery animal.

Wetness coats my face, my chin, and cheeks, making them shiny with her juices. I smile, glad I gave her such pleasure, and stiff beyond words with my own arousal.

She sighs in content, wiping a hand over my face. "I think I just rode your face like a carousel horse."

I chuckle and reach down to adjust my painful erection. "And I enjoyed every second of it."

"Are you worried I'll forget about your turn?" She settles her toned ass on my chest, sitting sideways, her legs trailing toward the floor. One hand skims across my denim clad thigh, brushing close to the open fly.

"Nope. That thought never crossed my mind." And truly, it hadn't. We've never played games of withholding pleasure from one another like punishment. We've dragged it out for hours for our mutual benefit, with no complaints from either side.

"Good!" She scoots off me and rises to her feet. I groan at the look of determination on her grinning face. "I'm not done taking pictures."

Chapter Nine

Heather

Tony is incredibly patient, allowing me to take pictures as long as I want. Every few minutes I nuzzle his thick dick behind his underwear or stroke over the fabric to keep him primed and ready. His low groans of arousal and heated stares are enough to keep me warm with nothing on but my stockings.

It felt empowering to ride his attentive tongue and take what I wanted, knowing all the while he was on the edge of control, eager to plunge inside me and race for his own finish. Talk about self-control. That man has it.

I'm not so sure if the situation were reversed I'd behave as well. Considering I mounted my lover's face and demanded an orgasm, it's probably a safe bet to say no, I wouldn't behave as well.

A glance at the camera's display reveals I've taken several hundred pictures of Tony so far. I can hardly wait to put them on a contact sheet and examine them. Without a doubt, half a dozen will be mounted on my bedroom wall if I have anything to say about it.

"That's it. We're done. I think I've tortured you long enough." I set down the camera and stalk toward my lover. "You were an absolute saint to be so patient. Thank you."

Naked desire slides over Tony's face as he silently lowers his jeans. "No more pictures, right?"

I nod, an impish grin on my face. "That's right. What did you have in mind?"

He hooks his thumbs into the waistband of the tight briefs and shoves the fabric over his hips. "I've got one last surprise for you."

My mouth drops open in a silent O as his cock springs free, revealing black leather circling the base of his shaft and strips of the same leather dividing his balls.

"Holy hell. Is that the cock ring from my apartment?"

Tony wraps a hand over his shaft and pumps. "Yup. I've had it on for hours." His voice sounds low and near the edge. "Hours." His fist slides back and forth. "Imagining when you'd see it... and how it would feel while I was inside you."

Arousing heat washes over my exposed flesh. Damn, he's freakin' hot. His prick looks naughty, like a weapon. A weapon promising hot sex. And damn, I want some of that.

"I want to watch as I slide deep inside you," he continues. "I want to see the hint of leather while I feel it wrapped around me."

My breath hitches. "You've had it on for a really long time. Does it hurt?"

His answering smile is wicked. "Nope. I adjusted it to barely fit, just in case it hurt. The only discomfort I'm in is from blue balls." His hand slows on his cock. "I need you now, woman. Are you ready? It's going to be hard and fast." He takes two steps closer, the hairs on his thighs tickling the skin above my thigh high stockings.

"I'm ready."

His chest heaves in fast pants. He scoops me up effortlessly and carries me to the chaise. In a flash, I'm on my back, my shoulders propped up on the armrest, with my legs spread wide and high. Tony kneels on the lounger, aiming his engorged flesh right where it needs to go.

His features are tense as he plunges inside me, driving his ringed-cock deep on the first stroke. Two strong hands press my thighs wider as my body stretches to accommodate him.

"You feel so good..." he says in a hoarse rasp of sound. "Hot. Wet. Tight." He's gazing down, where we're joined. "Look at us, Heather. Look at how sexy this is."

I lean forward slightly to do as he bids. The black leather circling his shaft draws my eye as he pumps slowly back and forth. He pulls out so far the head comes into view briefly, before he pushes back inside. I try to wiggle my hips, circle them to meet his thrusts, but his strong hands hold me firmly in place.

"Fucking hot," I say between pants. "I see the tight leather surrounding you."

"Touch yourself, baby. I want to watch you stroke your pussy."

Eager to join him when he comes, I slide one hand down to do as he asks. Instantly I'm edging up the hill toward release, sure the constant arousal I felt while taking pictures has left me as primed to come as he is. I dip my fingers lower, bracketing his cock to coat them with wetness. When he presses deep I feel the scrape of leather against them.

Sufficiently lubed, I reach higher, working myself like a mad woman. The thrust and withdrawal of his thickness feels out-of-this-world intense.

"Yeahhh... that's it. Play with that little clit." His fingers squeeze my thighs. "Make yourself come all over me."

His rhythm increases, losing some of its early finesse for sheer strength and speed. Sweat drips from his brow onto my stomach. He's staring where our bodies meet, closing his eyes now and then as if the sight is too much for him.

"I'm there, Heather. I'm gonna come."

His words elicit a deep, primal response in me. The muscles gripping him spasm tighter, pushing me to my release.

A loud moan rips from his throat, transforming mid-sound into a guttural shout. He pauses mid-stroke, holding still while his orgasm hits.

"More," I call out. "More, please!"

He thrusts again, deeper, slower, as my body convulses around his hardness. Mindless noises spill from both of us as we crest together, my own peak drawing out endlessly, wave after wave of pleasure suffusing me.

Tony releases my thighs and leans forward, nuzzling my lips for a soft kiss.

"Is it me," he whispers, "or does it seem like each time is better than the last?"

I wrap my arms around him and sigh. "I think you're right."

After we eat languidly and shower, we cuddle naked in his big bed. Unbidden, my earlier encounter with Jimmy surfaces. I relay the incident to Tony, hoping for his opinion on what to do.

"I'm not really good at this kind of thing. Guys tend to punch when an asshole deserves it. But I realize that's not a viable course in the workplace." He runs a hand through his hair, deep in thought. "I could come by and put the fear of God into him if you'd like."

"No. Thanks." The idea of a new lover confronting an old one almost sends me into a panic attack. "I'd like to handle this professionally, but don't want to come across as weak to my bosses."

Tony shrugs. "Complaining of harassment of any kind in the workplace isn't an indication of weakness. This is work we're talking about. You need to be able to function free of intimidation."

I sigh, and reach for my wine glass on a nearby tray. "You're right. I know it. I just didn't want to call attention to myself right away." The glass is empty, eliciting another sigh, this one of frustration.

Tony grabs the glass and his own. "No worries, mine needs a refill, too." He leaves the room, naked as the day he was born and uncaring of his disrobed state.

Then again, if I had his body I'd probably do the same thing.

Tony's phone vibrates on his nightstand. I lean over and look at the screen, checking to see if it's an Apollo number and if I should call him back to answer it. The name *Portia* and a number appears, but no picture. I don't recognize her name from the people Tony has mentioned at his old job, so I leave it be.

I settle back against the pillows, unable to completely let the call go despite my best intentions. Who is this woman that she'd phone late on a Friday night expecting Tony to answer? Could she be an old conquest looking for a booty call? I know he dated a lot of women before me, that was never something he could have hidden even if he tried. His picture was plastered all over the society pages way too often in the past five years.

Tabloid dramas aside, should I be worried? After this evening, my gut says no. There's no way all he's done for me could be anything similar to what he's done in the past for ex-girlfriends. He's complained they were often after his money, angled for diamonds, or badgered him for expensive getaways. So far nothing we've shared has been like that. And I've never asked for a thing from him.

Tony returns with our drinks in one hand and a small plate holding four chocolate covered strawberries in the other. Awww... so sweet. I think after he and I enjoyed them on our first date they will always be my favorite. He sets my drink on the nightstand closest to me and climbs back on the bed.

Say something! Tell him about the call. Let him explain.

My heart clenches in my chest. What if this woman does matter? Do I really want to hear about it tonight after all we've shared? I push the thoughts away and smile, determined to enjoy the effort he's made with the dessert.

"I don't think I'll ever look at a strawberry again without thinking of you and that picnic in your living room."

A blush heats my cheeks as I recall my bold and daring commands of that night. The Heather of today is a mixed version of her and the real me. More confident, yes, and ready to experiment, without a doubt. I'm growing each day, despite this new twist with Jimmy at Parkerson. I'm a stronger me—ready for a stronger man in my life. And that man is Tony.

Decision made, I refrain from informing him his phone rang when he was in the kitchen.

I need to trust him as much as he's trusted me. I know my heart is safe with Tony.

Late Saturday morning Tony nudges me out of bed.

"Come on... let's do a little shopping."

I reluctantly allow him to pull me into the shower, I was perfectly content to stay naked all darn day. Intrigued by the offer to shop, which most guys hate, I somehow manage to resist the soapy temptation to make love again under the warm spray. Damn, that man can be persuasive when he wants to be.

I dress in my clothes from yesterday, feeling slightly awkward to be in work clothes on the weekend. But hey, he did offer shopping so perhaps I can pick up something casual at a store nearby. I bet I could rock these shoes with a pair of jeans. We ride the elevator down and Tony draws the keys from his pocket, jingling them in one hand. Once we step outside he presses a button on the remote and an alarm sounds in the convertible I admired yesterday, still parked at the curb.

"New car?" I ask.

"Not quite. Has close to seven thousand miles on it."

I raise an eyebrow. "Exactly how many cars do you have?"

Tony shrugs a shoulder. "Why does that matter? My little brother sells cars. I like to support him." Brushing it off like it's nothing to own multiple vehicles, he offers me the keys. "Feel like driving? Someone wore me out last night and this morning."

"Ha! You're the one who offered to go shopping, not me." I smile and look over the shiny blue car. It sure is pretty. "And if I recall right, you weren't complaining last night or this morning, mister."

He dangles the fob from one finger, tempting me with the BMW dealership emblem catching the light. "Sure as hell I wasn't. That would be just plain stupid. And let me clarify my shopping offer so I don't lose my man-card: Lowes and grocery shopping."

I give in to the offer to drive his luxury vehicle, snatching the keys from his finger. "I knew there had to be a catch. No guy spontaneously offers to go clothes shopping with a woman."

He leans in to draw me closer. "That depends. Are we talking lingerie shopping? If yes, then I can be very spontaneous." A memory flits over his face. "Or shoes." His hands slide down my back to rest on my skirt-covered bottom. "I do like shopping for shoes with you."

I laugh, wiggling free from his grasp and walk to the driver's side door. "In case you've failed to notice, I do need a change of clothes." I open the door and slide inside. In a moment he joins me. "And since I'm driving, I say we stop for jeans first."

He smiles at me indulgently as I start the car. "You're the boss, babe. Whatever you want."

Chapter Ten

Tony

We spent the rest of the day together and all Saturday night. Cooking, laughing, and falling into each other's arms whenever the urge hit. The new jeans Heather picked hugged her sweet little ass, making it hard to keep my hands off her.

She was a good sport in the home improvement store, taking the time to let me choose the cabinetry for my next project, a home office. Very subtly, I'd get her opinion on colors and finishes, hoping to have her contribute a little to the space I'm creating. It might eventually make her more comfortable at my place and lead to more time here. Well, the photo studio will probably be the best enticement to that end.

On Sunday she went home to attend a yoga class with Carla and Katrina, who is another friend I met briefly at the bar a few weeks ago. It was the easiest thing in the world to pretend the car service wasn't available 'til much later and offer for her to take the blue convertible.

She grumbled about finding parking until I gave her the address of a garage a block from her building, not adding I'd recently secured a prime spot for her just two days ago. Having a car in the city can be expensive, but giving her the means to visit me in Jersey whenever she wants is more important to me than the cost.

I ignored my cell all weekend—which is now dead— uncaring if an emergency from Apollo crept up or not. They need to get used to solving shit on their own regarding the deals I've left behind. It felt nice to completely disconnect for a change. Besides, my family has the number to the landline if anything major happened with someone.

How will Heather react to my loud relatives? The last time I saw them was Easter dinner at my Aunt Rosa's, which means we're due for a get-together soon. Should I talk to her about meeting my mom and brothers first? Wonder if either cheeky bastard is seeing a girl right now. Might help divert attention off me and Heather if one of them brought someone, too.

Is meeting them too soon? Will she like being involved with a loud, overbearing Italian family? She's an only child and she told me her folks died in a car accident. No mention of any cousins. I'll have to ask.

I shake my head as I plug in my cell to charge. Christ. Me—worrying about introducing a girl to my immediate family. What's next, picking out china patterns? I shudder at the domestic thought.

After a minute the phone has enough charge and the unit powers on. Immediately it pings with voice mail and text notifications. I settle onto the couch and check the texts first, unwilling to let my Sunday good mood become spoiled with old work issues left via voice mail.

First one is a group message to me, Gino, and my other brother Vinnie, from Marcus yesterday: *We on for poker tomorrow? If yes, when and where?*

Gino responded with, *Yeah, I'm in. Tony's turn to host. I'll text the others. Meet at 6?*

Shit. I forgot all about the rotating poker game. I don't always make it anyway, usually working on my building or in the office. *Or partying in Vegas with your latest conquest.* I cringe at the accuracy of the statement when applied to last month and every month before that. Man whore. Yup. It fit all right.

Not anymore though. Turned over a new leaf with Heather. And she's worth it. Dark-eyed temptress with legs that never end and a mouth that never quits. Good thing we didn't make any plans for later, or I'd be scrambling to appease the guys when I bowed out.

I can hear Marcus's snarky voice in my head if I had tried to cancel due to a woman. *"Hos before bros? What the fuck is wrong with you?"*

Love is a tricky beast. I want to spend every waking moment with her, preferably wrapped in her arms with my cock buried deep inside her welcoming heat. But at the same time, I'm cognizant that the intense feelings could be one-sided and forcing myself on her too much could scare her away.

She's got the car. It's not like I won't see her again soon. She smilingly complained her muscles were sore from our nocturnal activities. Thanks to those aching muscles, she's going to be thinking about me even if I'm not right up in her face twenty-four seven. Time to chill and relax a little bit. Perhaps up the slow seduction with a lavish evening out to a play or show this week.

I text back to the guys that we're on for tonight and I'll order pizza. Next I open my laptop and search for what's playing in the theater district. It's possible to go to a show during the week and not stay out too late. Besides, a smile curves my lips at the idea, she might invite me to stay over at her place if it's late enough.

Finally, unable to put it off any longer, I check my voice mail messages. There are three from Portia. Each one growing in intensity, her desperation clear in the last voice mail.

"Please, Tony. I know I've been a bitch. Your lawyer has already contacted me. I get it. You don't want this baby with me. But we really need to talk. I'm torn on what to do... about the baby."

That sounds ominous. Like she's debating doing something drastic, like terminating the pregnancy. Considering I don't even know if the baby, assuming there really is one, is mine, I'm not sure what I should be doing or saying to influence her. It's her body, and ultimately her decision.

Guilt and responsibility weighing heavily on my heart, I return her call.

She answers right away. "Tony! I'm so glad you called. How are you doing?"

"Cut the small talk, Portia. I got your messages." I sigh, running a hand through my hair in frustration. "Fine. We'll talk in person."

"Great. I'll meet you for lunch tomorrow. Lobby of my parent's office building? Then we can go wherever you'd like."

She's being way too accommodating, which has me worried.

"Yeah, that's fine. See you then." I end the call, bile churning in my stomach.

More than anything I want this mess over and done with. I hate keeping it from Heather. Maybe I need to come clean sooner rather than later to make sure this doesn't bite me in the ass. It'll be weeks before a DNA test can be performed, and there's no way I want secrets between us for that long. They could easily fester and get blown way out of proportion.

You may be the father of another woman's unborn child. Don't you think that's beyond festering and overreacting?

I drop my head back on the couch, tension and unease forming a tight band across my forehead.

Damn it. I've got to tell her.

"Call," Tommy says, tossing two more chips into the middle. "Let's see what you've got, you dago bastard." Tommy works with Gino at the dealership, has for years. Not sure if he's still in sales or does something else now. He chugs the last of his beer, a rosy glow to his ruddy complexion. It clashes nicely with his short red hair.

Gino laughs at his buddy's bigoted slam while placing his winning hand on the dining room table. "Three tens. Read 'em and weep, you drunken mick."

Marcus nudges me with his elbow, prompting me to reveal my hand, too. "Wake up, man." He glances at his watch. "It's not that late."

I toss my losing cards on the table. After two nights in a row with little sleep and an unwelcome lunch date to look forward to tomorrow, it's safe to say my mind isn't on cards.

The sound from the baseball game blasting in the living room increases, the crowd reacting to a recent play.

"Did you see that?" Hank shouts. He's Tommy's ex-roommate from college. From what Gino tells me, both guys are single and slobs — having no idea their bad habits are *why* they're still single. It'll take a miracle for them to change. "Haven't seen Jeter hustle with any spirit since last season."

Tommy rises for a fresh beer, nodding toward my empty bottle to see if I want another. I nod back. "Thanks."

"What's eating you, man?" Marcus asks me. "I venture all the way out here to your *slum* in Hoboken." At my darkening look he hastily adds, "Which, I will concede, is much nicer than I anticipated. You showed me around. I oo'd and ahh'd at all the appropriate times regarding your construction prowess—so what gives? Why are you so quiet? Trouble in paradise?"

I shoot him a shut-the-fuck-up look, which he ignores.

He wiggles his eyebrows. "Portia giving you a hard time?"

Marcus smiles at my glower, knowing full well I'd like to kick his ass for bringing up her name in front of these guys.

Gino gathers up the cards to shuffle for another round. "I thought the girl you're dating was named Heather. Who's this Portia chick?"

Vinnie, my middle brother, is in the kitchen, whipping up some munchies with whatever he can find. "Hold on now. Did I just hear you right? Big brother has a steady girl and no one thought to tell me? What the fuck is up with that?"

I resist punching Marcus, but it's a close call. "Yes, on dating Heather. No on dating Portia."

Vinnie laughs from the island, a big knife in one hand. "Classic! Wait 'til Mom hears about this. You are going to bring her by for Sunday dinner next week, right? Better do it quick before Aunt Rosa finds out and beats Mom to a big family event you'd *have* to attend—with a date."

Tommy strolls in with our beers, setting mine down and then taking his seat. "Isn't Portia the one you took to

Vegas like two months ago? Hank, wasn't she the girl on the jet who offered to blow you in the bathroom?"

Hank sputters into his beer, a look of outrage on his face. "Damn, asshole. Why'd you have to bring that up? She was drunk and didn't mean it. I told her no and steered her back to her seat."

Unsurprised at the revelation, after all, she was a party girl, I ask, "And where was I when this happened?"

Gino deals the next hand, watching each of us for signs the interchange could turn physical. We've known each other for years, it sure as hell wouldn't be the first time.

Geez. What a joke. Like I'd lift a finger to defend a woman who's angling to squeeze me for millions.

"You were asleep in the back bedroom," Tommy answers. "Complained of an early morning meeting if I'm recalling right."

"Yeah, I remember now. That was Portia. She's a real piece of work. The Vegas trip was our last weekend together."

"And?" Gino prompts. "Why would she be giving you a hard time now? You broke up a while ago."

I glare at Marcus, wishing I really could punch him hard for opening his big mouth. Maybe when the others leave I'll get a chance. "She's been calling me." I stare down my college friend, silently promising him bodily harm if he opens his trap again.

Marcus wears a look of innocence, trying to play off he meant no harm. Sure. Rat bastard. Punk loves to stir up shit when he can. He grabs his beer and takes a long drink.

"Considering you just bought Heather a BMW, you should probably ignore Portia's calls," Gino says. "Just saying. Not worth trying to juggle two women. Trust me."

Marcus spews beers across the table. "What the hell? You bought her a car? Are you insane?"

My blood boils. Why the hell did I agree to this game? What the devil was I thinking having these meatheads over to my place? They're such pains in the asses. Bunch of yentas. Gabbing and gossiping once they get bored with sports talk.

I examine my cards, refusing to rise to their bait. "Don't recall asking you asshats how to spend my hard-earned savings. Can we get back to the game?"

Hank ignores my dark look and presses on. "When do we get to meet her? Sounds pretty serious if you gave her a car."

"What does she look like?" Tommy asks. "You seem to date a wide *variety* of types."

I discard the crap cards and hold onto the only viable ones I've been dealt. Answering them will only lead to more questions, so I ignore them. When the insults and hidden jabs get to be too much, you can never show it. Guys revel in picking each other apart with verbal slams, looking for a weakness. They're like sharks in a crowded backyard pool. At the first hint of blood, you're dead.

Tossing three chips into the pot, I open the first round of betting.

There's no way I'm talking about Heather in front of these jokers. They'll never let it go. And I'd much rather allow what we have to grow in private than risk it being tainted by these jerks.

I shoot Marcus a look that clearly says *payback is a bitch*. I may not know when, but I'll return the favor.

Chapter Eleven

Heather

It's Monday, almost noon, and I've seen Jimmy stop by Tammy's cube twice. I hesitate on whether to share my thoughts about the man with her. Would my negative opinion be welcome? Judging by the happy smile on her face, I'd say probably not.

If I tell her he's a two-timing womanizer would that come across as slanderous? Or perhaps I could say he treats women poorly. Would that be enough info or would she ask me questions? More than likely, they'd be ones I don't want to answer.

Crap, I really wish this stuff was easier. I've never had someone work for me before, even temporarily. Maybe I should invite her out to lunch and attempt a girls chat then. That might work. Ugh.

I know putting it off isn't the wisest choice... but really, I don't know the woman all that well and she might resent my interference. Surely a woman with half a brain would see through his charming veneer?

Uh, yeah. Like you did?

Okay, good point. I'll talk it over with Carla at lunch. Hopefully she has better ideas than I've been able to come up with.

I gather up my cell and purse and head out the door. I catch a glimpse of Tammy leaving with two women and a tight band of pressure I was unaware of loosens in my chest. At least she's not having lunch with him. Yet.

In a few minutes I'm striding down the sidewalk, letting the mid-day spring sun warm me. My cheeks heat as I recall the sunlight coloring Tony on Friday in my new studio. Geez, he's incredible. I wander to my destination, content with the glow of memories from that night. Oh, and then Saturday. Yum.

"Heather! Over here!" Carla's booming voice carries across our favorite lunch place.

I weave through the crowded establishment and settle into a chair across from her.

"Have you been waiting long?" I ask.

"Nah, just got here a few minutes ago. The place filled up fast."

"How have you been?"

"Not bad, busy. Traveling again next week, I think."

"Where to this time?"

"Probably upstate, not too far. Oh hey, I just saw—"

She stops as our waitress arrives. The college-aged woman fills our water glasses and takes our orders. As she bustles away, I look to Carla with raised eyebrows. "What were you about to say? Something you saw?"

"You said Tony left Apollo, right?"

I nod, wondering where she's going with this. "Yeah, beginning of last week."

"Well, I saw him near my office building getting into a taxi with a brown-haired woman." She looks concerned, possibly remembering my issue with Jimmy cheating on me and the subsequent fallout of picking up the pieces of my heart again. "Could he be going on a job interview?" Her tone rises with hope.

My stomach drops, fear making me wonder if her un-voiced worry might be accurate. He could be going on a lunch date. After all, Tony and I never said we'd be exclusive. "What did she look like?"

Dammit! I can't believe I asked that. What could her looks possibly matter?

Maybe you want your best friend to reassure you you're more attractive than her. Pathetic.

I saw some of the skanks Jimmy cheated on me with, I doubt looks had anything to do with his decision. More like they were female and said yes.

"I didn't get a good look at her besides her hair—shiny brown and chin length. My vague first impression was one of put-together and fashionable. But not Tony. That's another story."

"What do you mean?"

"He looked angry or *really* unhappy. Had a nasty grimace on his face. Like he was ready to scream in frustration. I thought maybe she was an annoying client or co-worker, and then I remembered he left Apollo. That's what made me think of the interview idea—but his face didn't match."

"At least it doesn't sound like a mid-day tryst." I release a breath I hadn't known I was holding.

Carla's eyes widen in alarm. "Cheating on you? You really thought that was an issue? Tony might have appeared like a ladies man when we first met him, but I never pegged him as the cheating type."

I shrug, twisting my napkin in both hands. "Aren't they kind of the same?"

"Hell no! There's flirty and appreciative and then there's slimy, underhanded, and two-timing. Very different beasts and they shouldn't be confused as the same."

"You're right. I think I'm projecting." I straighten in my chair, eager to get it off my chest. "Jimmy, my ex, was hired at Parkerson. I think he has designs on me, somehow—but I don't know why, or even how."

"What?!? When the hell did this happen? Why didn't you tell me right away? Damn girl, I bow out of yoga one week because of cramps and I miss everything!"

I smile at her reaction. "I still think you should have come anyway. Yoga would have helped. But don't worry, I wouldn't have said anything in front of Katrina anyway. She doesn't know about what I went through back then and I'd rather not re-hash it all."

"Yeah, I hear you. Let past issues stay in the past, I understand. I always admired how you never let Jimmy's infidelities color how you approached relationships with other men. That could have messed up a lesser woman for *years*. But holy cow, what are you going to do? And of course you're right. He's there for a reason. Slimy prick. You should have let me spray paint 'CHEATER' on his apartment door. Hah! Bet that would have put a crimp in his whoring."

I smile. God, it's good to have friends like Carla. "That would have been fitting. I should have agreed." At the time I wanted to be free of him and lick my wounds. Now I wish I'd retaliated in some way. Childish? Yup, but there it is.

I fill her in on everything that's occurred with Jimmy, limited though it may be. She listens in silence, our food arriving near the end of my recounting.

Carla grabs the pepper churn for her salad. "Are you going to say anything to your assistant Tammy? I think she deserves a warning."

"And what would I say? 'Hey, you might want to avoid that asshole. I dated him and he cheated on me. Oh, he also systematically broke down my confidence, leaving me a shattered woman.' That's a great thing for me to have spread through the office."

"Okay, I agree. That doesn't sound like the best phrasing to start with. And besides, who's being dramatic now? You weren't shattered, just bent a little. Come on— man up, buttercup. You've got to say something. Wouldn't you want someone to have told you about him?"

I've never been a fan of confrontation, especially in the workplace. I mentally back-pedal. "Maybe I'm over-reacting to the situation."

Coward.

Carla forks in a mouthful of salad, an indignant expression crossing her face. After chewing and swallowing she says, "No. You're not. Trust your gut. How did you and Jimmy finally end things?"

I push my salad around with a fork. "I went home from work sick and walked in on him screwing someone from his office in my new bed. Threatened to call the cops and then managed to chase them both into the hall, semi-naked, while I was waving the phone like a madwoman. Packed up all his personal stuff— and their clothes— tossed everything into the hall. He yelled at me the whole time, shouting about all the other women— geez, even my hairstylist— he'd screwed during our relationship. Blaming me for being so bad in bed he had to turn elsewhere."

"I could never forget *that* incident. We commiserated about it for weeks. Polished off a lot of wine and tequila if I'm recalling correctly. We threw out the whole sheet set and went shopping for new stuff—even pillows and a mattress cover." She smiles and takes a sip of water. "At least I convinced you not to burn the mattress." Carla reaches across the table and touches my arm briefly. "What I meant was, did you ever see or talk to him after that day?"

I shake my head. "He tried. I refused. What more was there to say?"

"Hmmm... and now over a year later—"

I interrupt, "Eighteen months."

She glares at me with a look that says *yeah, but who's counting* before continuing, "He takes a job at your office. I dunno. It doesn't feel right. And the whole misdirection with asking about Tammy's relationship status? I have no idea what he's up to."

"Me either. Could he have changed? Maybe he's really interested in her. Should I give him the benefit of the doubt and stay out of it?"

"You can do whatever you want. But me? I'd be ready for the worst. Guys like him don't ever *really* change. I wouldn't put it past the asshole to either try and get you back or set out to ruin your relationships at work."

"All right," I say, a hint of determination creeping back in, "I'll be on the look-out for slimy, underhanded tactics from the ex-boyfriend in the workplace. Now what do I do about Tony? Do I say anything about the woman you saw him with? It could be nothing... it could be something."

"It'll be hard to bring up without mentioning me. Not that I mind, but accusations—as well as polite inquiries—are best done with first-hand knowledge. What if I'm wrong and it wasn't him?"

"I guess you're right. It would sound really odd saying you saw him with a strange woman. And very high-schoolish. Like I didn't trust him. After all, he is a grown man. He doesn't need to report his everyday actions to me."

"And he's given you no reason to doubt him, has he?"

I hesitate, my mind immediately going back to that phone call when he was refilling our wine. "Well, he did get a call from a woman named Portia last Friday night. He was out of the room and didn't know she called."

"Girl! Why didn't you tell me that before? Of course that's important. Did you answer it?" Carla asks, brows raised in curiosity.

"No! I just happened to lean over casually... and quickly read the name on his screen. You know, before he came back and caught me."

She chuckles. "I bet that would have been funny to see. Did Tony check his phone later or leave to return the call? Don't jump to conclusions because of Jimmy."

"Nope. As a matter of fact, he didn't pick up his cell at all. It was refreshing. Just the two of us with no distractions. All night. All day Saturday. And even into Sunday."

"That doesn't sound like a guy who's got a girl on the side. You told me Jimmy used to get texts at all hours, and he'd take 'business' calls out of earshot all the time. I think Tony's on the up and up." She pauses, considering. "But... I know you. If it doesn't resolve, you're going to let it stew and eat away at your new found self-confidence." She smiles to ease the harsh appraisal. "Hell, we can't let that happen. I really like the new you. Sassy and sexy." She winks. "A little like me, only with a steady guy instead of playing the field."

Her remark is the perfect opening to mention my own concerns about her casual approach to relationships, but I refrain. The timing isn't right and I'm still unsure if saying anything to her would help or not. But I will, soon. I owe it to her as a friend, despite how I feel about confrontations.

We finish our lunches and say our goodbyes, the whole situation weighing on me more than it should. Could the woman Tony met be Portia? And if yes, what do I do about it?

Chapter Twelve

Tony

The upscale restaurant Portia picked for lunch was the same place I took her on our first date. A fact I didn't remember until she pointed it out to me. She's dressed to entice in a low cut blouse and snug riding pants to show off her curves. No trace of pregnancy mars her flat middle. Yet.

The initial flirting in the cab ended when I removed her hand from my arm and now she's settled on behaving more business-like. No trace of the sad, confused woman who left me a message, implying she might do something drastic.

I knew I couldn't be so lucky as to have her decide to terminate the pregnancy on her own. Inwardly I cringe at my own selfishness. I admit, with my Catholic background, the mere idea of ending an unwanted pregnancy when you're healthy, have the means to support the child, and are over the age of twenty had me picturing all my aunts and Mom screeching and spouting their pro-life opinions at me again. That was certainly the dumbest discussion I ever brought up over dinner—and one I will never attempt again.

Unable to eat while listening to Portia's plans and demands, I stare at the food on my plate, wondering what the hell I've done to deserve this situation. Was it dating too much? Living life a little *too* carefree? Treating women like temporary adornments, meant to be exchanged on a whim?

Yeah, that might be it.

"Don't you think setting up a trust fund would be the easiest?" Portia's voice pulls me out of my musings. "I could be the executor and make sure all the child's needs are met."

Acid roils in my gut. I can't say what's on my mind. It would be too crass and rude to yell what a greedy bitch she sounds like.

"*Don't you think* you're jumping the gun a little bit, Portia? You've got a positive test result confirmed. That's it. There's still no scientific proof the child is mine."

The slim woman smiles, her dark blue eyes tightening at the corners. "Yet. It's yours, Tony. Might as well start planning for it."

"Forgive me if I don't go willingly to slaughter."

Her light laughter tinkles on the air between us. "Slaughter? Don't you think that's a bit dramatic? I thought women were the ones to hold the corner on such rantings."

My hands fist on my thighs. She's right. I am being a wuss about all of it. But at the same time, I refuse to be pushed into discussing details of child support until the DNA results come back.

"Let's call a truce, Portia."

She raises an elegant eyebrow. "Isn't that what we're doing here?"

I shake my head slowly. "No, not really. The past week you've vacillated from cajoling, to seducing, to even sounding vaguely threatening during our minimal exchanges. And now, here you are, ready to sit down and plan out this baby and my financial involvement—way before we should." I relax my hands and reach across the table to take one of her tiny hands in mine. "I know it's hard to hear, and I do promise to respond more maturely when you call or when you want to discuss things in person—but only after we have proof the baby is mine."

Her face hardens, but she nods briefly, once. "I understand. I don't like it. But I understand." Her eyes moisten but thankfully no tears fall. "Can you at least tell me why you won't give us a second chance?"

Not wanting to mention Heather, I stick to the truth without her in it. "After our fling ran its course, I realized I didn't have deeper feelings for you." A tear slides down her face and I rush to soften the blow. "We had a great time. But we didn't really click." I glance away, realizing I'm still not helping her feel better. "It wouldn't be fair to you, me, or a baby, to continue. We'd wind up hating each other. Which would be an awful situation for a child to grow up in."

She turns her hand over and grips mine tightly, her voice broken and teary. "We could have made it work. Lots of people do."

I sigh and squeeze her hand back. "You deserve better in life than settling for less than real love. And so do I."

She pulls her hand from mine and wipes her eyes on the edge of her cloth napkin. "Okay. We'll try it your way." A glint of the old Portia shines in her eyes, perhaps drowned out temporarily by all the added hormones. "For now."

After lunch, I'm unsure where to go and wander the streets, seemingly aimless, until I find myself near Central Park. I enter at the south end, meander to the pond near West 59th and Fifth Avenue, and lower myself to a bench, content to stare across the water and think.

When I look back on how I've handled things with Portia, I'm appalled. It was like I was so angry to be put in the situation that common decency escaped me entirely. Could she have been after my money? Well, yes, and she still could be, but did I have to react the way I did? Accusatory and defensive. Nice.

Gandhi once said you could learn a lot about a civilized society by how they treat their animals, and yet here I've been treating a woman I slept with, with less respect than I would a pregnant cat.

Talk about humbling. And shitty.

I need to tell Heather. Tonight. No more excuses.

My phone rings and I dig it out of my pants pocket, unsure if I feel like talking to anyone. I recognize the number and answer.

"Mr. Carmine? It's Joseph, from J&R Investigations."

"Hi, Joseph. Good to hear from you. What do you have for me?"

"Not a lot, sir. We were able to dig up public information from the time frame you indicated. From it, we've confirmed at least two other single men she was seen with in public. But that's not proof she slept with them."

I grunt, the sound non-committal. "Go on."

"That's about it so far. Your situation is unique. Most cases we investigate are for people looking for current proof of an affair, not unsubstantiated possibilities from months prior."

"Did you find anything on men she might be seeing now?"

"No, sir. She dropped out of her normal social scene about two weeks ago— not going to clubs, charity galas, or lavish private parties."

"Okay, thanks. I want you to dig into her financials and report on her spending habits, too. Might lead to something we can use down the line."

We end the call and a part of me feels dirty. It seems underhanded to investigate Portia when there's no proof the baby is even mine. But on the other hand, being prepared for any merger—even one that's not between companies, but two hostile people—is logical. It's the only way I can go into this pregnancy negotiation and hold onto my sanity.

There's a buzzing in my chest, like thousands of wasps trying to fly their way free. It takes me a few minutes, but I finally figure out what it is—it's panic over the loss of control this entire situation has produced. I may feel like a douchebag for doing all the digging on Portia, but whether I like it or not, I apparently crave a sense of control—small though it may be.

I relax on the bench, consciously letting go of the perceived need to control, and watch the ducks, enjoying their languid swimming and occasional fluttering of wings. The sounds of spring—birds chirping, water splashing, and random shouts from hot dog vendors—fill the air around me.

Time tends to flow unaccounted and free when you're ruminating and looking deep within yourself. Before I know it, it's after five. I notice the change when foot traffic increases in the park. I stand and stretch—as ready as I'll ever be to tell Heather.

When Heather arrives at her place, I'm already seated at the dining room table, two glasses of wine in front of me.

"Tony—what a nice surprise. Did we have plans and I slipped up? I hope you weren't waiting on me long." She hangs up her purse and joins me at the table.

"You're good. We didn't have any plans. Sorry to show up unannounced like this, but I need to talk to you."

Panic flits across her face, to be replaced with wariness. "Is something wrong?"

I half stand and kiss her on the lips. "Not between us, darling. This is all my fault—something from my past."

She relaxes a bit and takes a sip from her wine. "Okay then, shoot."

I sigh and return to my seat, the pressure building in my chest now that I'm here and about to spill what I've been dreading to share. I'd rather hoped the pressure would lessen once I arrived. It hasn't. "You know I dated a lot of women before we met. I've never hidden that."

"It's not like you could—I do read the papers." She smiles slightly, possibly trying to reassure me to keep going.

"Well, this woman approached me last week. We dated a couple of weeks before I met you." I stare at the woman I'm falling in love with, my heart frozen momentarily in my chest. "She says... um... she's claiming to be pregnant with my child."

Heather stills, her face completely unreadable.

I bolt out of my chair and start to pace. "There's no proof it's mine, but I was 'with' her. I'm not denying that. And the timing fits with what she claims." I pass the kitchen and turn around, nervous energy inhibiting me from sitting still. "I don't believe it's mine. She was a party girl through and through. But I have no proof."

I realize I've started to repeat myself, but can't seem to stop babbling while I pace. "There's nothing I can do until there's a DNA test. But again, I doubt very highly it's mine."

I turn to look at my girlfriend, hoping to read something on her face.

Heather stares at the table, unable to meet my eyes. Uh-oh. That can't be good.

"I'm on the pill, that's the only reason we've had sex without a condom. You told me you hadn't had unprotected sex with anyone else in years."

I rush forward and grab her arms, forcing her to look at me. "I haven't! I didn't! I swear!" My breath pants out in gasps. "That's why I felt it was all a scam. I *always* used a condom. Until you. No way could it be mine."

"A scam? Isn't that a little harsh?"

Not proud of my previous thoughts, I still don't hide them from her. "You'd have to know her. She's always been out for a good time—parties a little harder than she should, comes from money, has a trust fund she pisses away shopping... it seemed like she latched onto me strictly for a good time. And so I could pay for whatever she desired past her monthly allotment." I drop her arms and run a hand through my hair, frustrated anew with Portia's past behavior. "I thought for sure it was all a lie... but she showed me her blood work today at lunch. A lab has confirmed she is indeed pregnant."

My heart feels like there's a fist wrapped around it, squeezing the very life out of me. "Please, say something."

"This doesn't make sense. You say she's rich and yet she's coming after you for what? Moral support?"

"Moral support." A unamused snort escapes me. "Yeah, no. At first she wanted us to get back together." Panic flares across Heather's face again. "Don't worry, I told her it wasn't ever going to happen. I don't care for her like that. Never did. Once I saw her true colors how could I?"

Heather's voice sounds hesitant. "Well, if she comes from money and you knew she was a party girl, then how were you surprised by her actions? Sounds to me like you got what you bargained for—and then got angry when your hand was caught in the cookie jar."

A frustrated sigh pours out of me. "I'm not explaining this well. Yes, her family has money and she has a trust fund. But she doesn't work, I feel she's husband shopping to live like she wants— and this pregnancy is the best way to do it."

She looks shocked. "You really think she'd do all this for *more* money? Just doesn't sound... realistic. I mean really, how much money are we talking about? Like it's that much more than what she has already?"

This is it. The moment I've dreaded since we met, but knew I couldn't avoid it if we wanted to have any kind of serious future together. I sigh and take her hands in mine. "Heather, I've done exceptionally well for myself in a very short period of time. My net worth—that's the apartment buildings, stocks, bonds, cars, boat, cash assets, the houses—"

"Houses?" she squeaks out.

"—is well over five hundred million dollars."

Chapter Thirteen

Heather

Utter silence fills the dining room as I stare into Tony's worried brown eyes.

"Say something, Heather. You're killing me."

I open my mouth to speak, but coherent thought escapes me. "I-I-I don't know what to say. That's more money than anyone I know could earn in a hundred life times. And here I thought I was doing well with contributing to my 401k, starting an IRA, and having a high five-figure nest egg in my various checking and savings accounts."

For not knowing what to say, that sure as hell was a lot of babbling. Fool.

"Can you see why I might have presumed the worst of Portia?"

Hearing him say her name confirmed what I was thinking when he mentioned seeing the blood results over lunch. She must have been the woman Carla saw him with. "Is that her name? Portia?"

He nods and looks away. "I'm sorry I didn't tell you sooner. I really thought she was playing me and wanted to handle it all on my own."

"What changed your thinking?"

"Seeing her. Seeing the lab report." He runs a hand over his handsome face, looking more haggard than I've ever seen him. "It made me realize this nightmare might become real and I had to tell you or risk losing you when it all came out."

"Oh, you were right. It's good you told me. Secrets like this could easily ruin any relationship. But... I... um... I'm sorry. I need some time to think about all this. It's a lot to spring on a girl."

The life drains out of him. "Oh. I see. Do you want me to go?"

I hesitate, torn over wanting to reassure him and needing to get my head on straight. I wish now more than ever my mom and dad were alive so I could talk to them. "Don't hate me when I say yes. I've had a long day and after this little impromptu confession, I'm feeling pretty wiped. So yeah, I just want to soak in the tub by myself and sort it all out."

"Sort what out? Does my money really make a difference between us?"

"It's not the money, Tony. I've never cared about that and you know it." I leave the rest unsaid. He's smart. He can figure out I mean the baby and how he's handling the situation—and from what he's said so far, it sounds like he's handling it poorly.

"I know you're not ready to talk to me yet, and I respect that. But maybe you should call a friend. Bottling it up can't be good for you."

"Yeah. Or you," I say with a wink. Without my parents to talk to I've learned to talk things out with friends. Maybe he's right and I should call Carla. Hopefully she's free. I do need to get this off my chest.

Out of nowhere he grabs me and kisses me, igniting my desire and growing love. His arms wrap firmly around me, desperation in their strength. After a moment he breaks the kiss, breathing heavy.

"It's this," he whispers. "What we feel for each other that matters above everything else." His hand trails over the hair hanging down my back. "I'll go—for now. But you're not getting rid of me so easily."

I smile, a small upward curve of the lips. "Good. I never thought that."

The moment Tony leaves I call Carla. "Can you come over for dinner and drinks? I need to talk."

"Sure thing, girlfriend, I've got nothing going on tonight. I'll be over in thirty. Want me to pick up Chinese?"

"That sounds great. I've got plenty of wine."

By the time eight thirty rolls around we've polished off most of the food and close to two bottles of wine. If I'm being honest, I probably drank most of the wine.

"What really has me concerned is his attitude in all this, you know?" I say. "Like this woman is out to get him somehow. He actually used the word 'scam' when telling me about Portia's pregnancy."

Carla shrugs and tops off our wine, killing the bottle. "In his defense, there are women like that. I don't know of any personally. In general, I prefer not to hang out with conniving women." She giggles. "Too much work. All that scheming and shit. I like my relationships simple. Easier to handle that way."

No matter how perfect of an opening this is to address the promiscuous behavior she exhibits in her relationships, I refrain. Considering the amount I've had to drink, I will undoubtedly muck it up. Yeah, and that conversation will require tact—and sobriety. I make a mental note to definitely say something next week. Or the week after. Maybe over coffee. Yeah, that's the ticket.

"Doesn't he come across as insensitive to you?" I ask. "I mean, like, the poor woman. He seems more wrapped up in what the baby will cost him than the fact he might become a friggin' father. What about her? Who's going to be there for her when she has the baby?"

"Hey now, drunk girl. Don't go projecting your own fears of being in the same situation—and alone—onto her. She has parents who support her financially, she has money, so she can hire help. Hell, if she initially snagged Tony for a date, you know she has got to have looks and possibly brains. Hopefully her parents sent her to a good college." Carla leans forward and annoyingly snaps her fingers in front of my face. "Snap out of it, Heather! You don't need to worry about her—you need to worry about you."

"Me?"

"Yes, you. Haven't you thought about how this affects you? Do you want to be involved with a man with this kind of baggage? If you stay with him, do you want to have another woman's kid in your life for the next eighteen years? Do you want to be involved in a relationship that contains a shrewish harpy who chases the almighty dollar on the premise of caring for a child?"

I stare at my blond friend, liking her hair more now that it's grown out a little from her previous pixie cut. "Doncha think you're being a little harsh?"

"Whatever." She gulps more of her wine. "I'm just calling it like I see it."

Dread settles in my middle and the wine sours. "Peachy. Thanks a lot."

"S-s-s-ooOooo?" she slurs the word. "Whacha you gonna do?"

I drink the rest of my wine, glad we didn't open another bottle. "I dunno. I'll have to think on it."

Carla snorts. "Damn skippy, you better." She stands and heads to the kitchen. "Have any chocolate in this dump?"

I'm late to work the next day, my eyes feeling like sandy glue was poured in them overnight and my stomach ready to rebel at a moment's notice. God, I'm a lightweight when it comes to drinking.

Could have been because you didn't each much dinner, genius.

Yeah, that could be it.

My morning went from bad to worse when Tammy told me she went on a date last night with the cute new sales guy, Jimmy. Ugh. I froze like a deer in headlights. Nodded my head and said something stupid like, "That's nice."

My inability to act has led to this. My fault. Totally. If I had said something to her earlier about what a sleaze ball he is, she could have avoided him, told him no, been safe from a broken heart. Instead, I did nothing.

What the hell are you doing? Is this some special take-the-blame-for-everything *kind of crap? She's a grown woman. You're not responsible for who she chooses to date.*

Sure. That's what I'll tell myself when she cries like I did.

The day passes in a mindless blur of numbers, various emails, and phone calls. I've fielded two texts from Tony. Both were gentle inquiries on his part, wondering if I was ready to talk and how my day was going. My responses were short and to the point, telling him I needed to focus on work and we'd talk later.

A baby. Holy crap. I'm not so sure talking it over with Carla last night made the situation any clearer. Do I want to help raise someone else's child? How do I feel about dealing with the wrinkle of Portia's inclusion in our lives?

The money really isn't my concern, but I see how in this case having money puts an entirely new spin on things. Could she sue him for millions in child support? How will he deal with that? Will it sour him to having kids again? And if yes, what does that mean for me?

This is real world stuff I hadn't bargained for when dating him. It would be nice if everyone you met had a clean slate with no history, no mistakes, no emotional baggage... but this situation Tony's in has become more and more common for people in their late twenties and early thirties.

People make mistakes. People fall in love with the wrong person. Then they wake up when the glow of lust has worn off and find themselves in a relationship with someone they don't really like or have much in common with. Hell, who am I to judge when I made a mistake with choosing Jimmy? No one is infallible. We all mess up relationships once in a while.

Does that mean people don't get a second chance? What would I have done if my birth control failed and I got pregnant with Jimmy's child? Would I have stayed with the womanizer out of fear of raising a child on my own? Carla doesn't truly understand the fear of shouldering that kind of responsibility when you literally have no family to turn to.

An email comes through on the company server, pulling me from my maudlin musings. It's from Oliver, telling me I need to go to Philly tomorrow to deal with the finer details of freeing up assets in one of our long term investments. This one requires board approval and that means, as the CFO, the job falls to me. Several meetings have been set up, the first a meet and greet breakfast at eight a.m.

I respond that I'll be there, inwardly grateful for the break it will grant from the recent personal dramas. I fire off an email to the travel liaison requesting a train ticket for tonight, returning tomorrow evening, and to book a hotel near the office building.

This work excursion will give me much-needed space to think. Does this business trip and my sudden enthusiasm to go mean I'm running from my current problems? I shake my head. Work is work. Tony shouldn't take it personally. He knows what it means to be ambitious and care about your job. I'll explain it when I talk to him again.

Before three thirty, I get an email back confirming a ticket to Philly for six p.m. I prepare what I need to take, shove it all and my tablet into my oversized bag, and leave, still having to head to my place and pack clothes. Early morning meetings are never fun, but I'm glad to be spending the night before the appointment. I won't be dealing with morning commuters from here to there at five a.m. to make the first meeting.

I head out, catching an elevator to the lobby while searching the weather on my phone to plan on what to wear.

A familiar, and unwelcome voice, jars me from my thoughts. "And where are you bustling off to before the work day ends?" Jimmy's voice slides over me, practiced and charming. "Secret meeting?" He wiggles his eyebrows.

A grimace twists my mouth as I keep walking. "Uh, no. Isn't that more your speed?" I fire off my response without thinking, the old resentment closer to the surface regarding his past trysts than I was aware.

He chuckles. "Can't help if the ladies can't resist me." He falls into step beside me, keeping pace despite my antagonistic remark.

Unbidden, my response spills out in haste. "Oh, was that the problem? I thought you had a faulty zipper and your dick kept falling out of your pants."

Laughter, sharp and loud, spills from him. "Good one. You've become more feisty. I like it."

I turn and stare at him, hesitating for a brief moment in my exit. "You *like it*? That's rich. I've grown up. You haven't. Back off. We're not at work and I don't have to be polite to you here." I storm out the revolving doors, anger and a tinge of fear lighting my nerves on edge. Will he yell at me like he did that day in the hall outside my apartment? Will he make a scene in public?

I turn back and glance at him briefly, catching sight of the speculative look on his face. At least he's not yelling. I hope to God he leaves me the hell alone.

Chapter Fourteen

Tony

Around six thirty a text comes through from Heather. The longest one I've received from her all day.

Have to go to Philly tonight for meetings tomorrow. On train now. I'll be back before five tomorrow. Want to get together for dinner?

Pressure eases in my chest. At least she wants to see me. That's got to be a good sign. But if I'm honest, I don't want to wait 'til then to talk to her. I debate what to write for a minute and then go with my gut.

Sounds good. Call me when you get into Philly.

Okay. Will do. :-)

"Was that Heather?" my brother Vinnie asks. He stopped by on his way home from the restaurant to pick up the coat he left on Sunday night.

"Yeah. How did you know?"

"You've got a goofy smile on your face. Wuss."

I slap him on the shoulder in passing. "You could be a detective. You're so smart." Opening the fridge, I ask, "Want a beer?"

"Sure, why not. I'm off tonight. Want to grab some dinner?"

I hand him a beer and then gesture at my full fridge. "I've got plenty here. How about we eat in?" I don't add that I shopped with Heather and over-bought in the hopes she'd be spending more time here.

"You just want me to cook for you, don't you?" Vinnie smiles, not focusing on me or the beer, but staring into the fridge, looking as if he's mentally cataloging what I've got.

"Only if you want. Believe it or not, I am self-sufficient. I do remember the tips you taught me after you graduated from the Culinary Institute—and all the recipes Mom drilled into us growing up."

"Fine. It'd be nice to have someone cook for me for a change."

He settles at the island as I select steaks, mushrooms, and broccoli from the fridge. "I'm going for simple. No comments from you, all right?"

"Whatever, man. It'll give me a chance to grill you over the girl." He smiles and takes a long swig of his beer. "How are things going with her? Do we get to meet her soon?"

A cold lump of dread settles in my middle. Just the thought of introducing Heather to my family while we're in the middle of this whole baby thing leaves me ready to puke. "Things are complicated."

"Meaning?"

I prep the veggies first, adding an onion from the cabinet to my tasks. "You remember Sunday when Marcus mentioned a woman named Portia?" At his nod, I continue. "Well... she's adding a level of complication to my life that might mess up my relationship with Heather. Turns out she might be pregnant with my kid."

Vinnie sputters and chokes on his beer, coughing to clear his airway. After a minute he's able to speak, red-faced and looking shocked. "Holy shit, Tony. How could you be so fucking stupid?"

I shake my head, while cutting the onions into slices. "Don't assume, man. I used protection. She's still claiming the child is mine."

"What are you going to do? Did you tell Heather?"

"I called a lawyer and a private detective. So far there's nothing the detective has found that I can use on her and the lawyer said we need to wait for a DNA test to do anything." I start the onions in a skillet and turn to wash the mushrooms.

"Hell. That's what you're in—pure Hell. Think it's payback for all those years flying to Vegas and banging any woman you wanted?"

I frown. "I wasn't like that. I worked hard and partied hard." I shrug. "What's wrong with that?"

"Why do you think I implemented the rule you couldn't date anyone from my restaurant? The first six months we were open I had more crying waitresses and under-chefs than any new business owner should ever have to deal with— and all thanks to you, you bastard. You left a string of broken hearts in your wake. "

"Did I? I never noticed."

He shakes his head and helps himself to another beer. "You've always been oblivious to the women around you—especially after you bag them. Wining and dining them, buying expensive trinkets, lavish trips—"

"Come on... since when is Vegas 'lavish'?"

"When you fly them out in a jet, asshole. How do you think these women survive after you lose interest? Serves you right you fall for one and your past comes back to bite you in the ass."

"I dump money-grubbing women and I'm the ass?" I ask while setting the steak in a hot pan to sear one side. I toss the mushrooms in with the sautéing onions.

"What? *You* make them fall for you with the special treatment, and then you wonder why they expect it from you later? You already got this new one a car—don't you think you're doing the same thing again, only on a grander scale? You should be thinking about your future responsibilities." He sits back down at the counter, a sour look on his face. "Jesus, what will Mom say when she hears you knocked up some woman and aren't going to marry her?"

I slam the saucepan full of broccoli on a burner and turn it on to boil. "What the hell? Marry her? Are you crazy? It might not even be mine."

"Oh, and I can guess what that means — you're probably freezing the poor girl out. Treating her like a gold digger. Not even thinking about the fact you might become a father." He watches me while I cook, anger fairly radiating off him. "Just like in high school. I picked up the pieces of the hearts you crushed back then, too."

A corner of my mouth lifts up at the memories he's slanting in his favor. "Yeah, and you never let them cry on your shoulder until their pants magically slipped off."

Vinnie begrudgingly agrees. "Maybe one or two times. But overall you broke more hearts than I took advantage of."

"I'm just making sure we're both recalling right and you aren't forgetting that you're no saint either."

He shrugs, taking particular interest in the meat. Staring at it in the pan. Probably worried I'm going to burn it. Nosy know-it-all chef. "Whatever. The past doesn't change the fact that I may be looking at a paternity suit to end all suits."

"Seriously? If it's your kid, you better grow up and stop acting like an asshole. I'm not saying you've got to marry someone you don't love, but you damned well better take your responsibility and man up. A child isn't something you casually take an interest in and toss aside when you're bored, like you did all those women. A child deserves more."

I don't answer and flip the steaks. Where is this anger from him coming from? I know I've treated women poorly in the past, but things aren't like that between Heather and me. How do I get him to understand I'm not the same guy and this isn't a casual relationship like the others?

Vinnie sighs and puts his beer down. "I've been meaning to say something for a while. But you and I... we don't have these types of talks much."

"I know—I was wondering where all this shit was coming from. Last time we talked seriously about women I think you were a senior in high school."

"Yeah, well... it needed to be said. You've been self-centered when it comes to women for years. The whole family caters to you: Mom, Gino, me... And I get it. You've worked your ass off to support us the moment you were old enough to get a job."

"Gee," I say while turning off the stove and dishing up our plates. "And you sound so grateful."

Vinnie takes the offered plate. "I voiced my gratitude then. I voiced it when you lent me money for my restaurant. But I will not stand by and listen to you babble some shit about what this baby may or may not do to you and your latest conquest."

I sit next to him at the counter, trying my best to rein in my desire to punch him, and listen to what he has to say. "Heather is not a conquest."

"Oh yeah, really? And what makes this one different?"

I take a long drink of my beer, chugging the rest before setting it on the counter. "Because I love her."

Vinnie is quiet for a few minutes, eating his meal in silence. When he finally speaks some of the anger I heard earlier is gone, replaced with empathy. "Well then, do you want her to see you handling this situation like a self-centered playboy used to slinging his dick around, or do you want to show her how a man owns up to his responsibilities with class and decorum?"

When Vinnie leaves I feel emotionally spent. Not a sensation I normally experience without a naked, sweaty Heather in the room with me. He's right. Which is humbling, to say the least. I knew I discarded women on a regular basis, but never before did I suffer consequences for it. They usually left me alone after the obligatory, brush-off diamond bauble.

Or maybe you just thought that tactic worked. Sounds like Vinnie knows firsthand it didn't.

Yeah, I probably shouldn't have dated his sous chef those two weeks after the restaurant opened. She was a really nice girl... just didn't hold my interest. No one's been able to do that, ever. And then along came Heather.

Sweet, spirited Heather. Who captured my heart one night on a wine bistro patio when she ordered me to get on my knees...

A shiver runs over my skin, tightening it, making me remember the spring night and her bold behavior. But if I'm honest, her actions weren't what won me. Her shy, and then tempting, dichotomies intrigued me. Made me look below the surface to see she had depth, fear, passion, and strength all the way to her toes.

She challenged my way of thinking and feeling those first few days—and everything about her from her shyly sexy smile to her enticingly decadent scent has stayed with me. Heather wormed her way under my skin without my ever being aware, and now... and now I could lose her based on how I've handled everything with Portia.

Damn if my brother wasn't right. A real man doesn't dodge something like this and act like he's the victim. Only a coward hides behind layers of people—lawyers, detectives, secretaries, receptionists—whatever, instead of facing the issue head-on.

What will I do if Portia is pregnant with my child? I've been so concerned with proving it's not mine and worried the news will affect my growing relationship with Heather, that I haven't looked inside and faced how I feel about the possibility of becoming a father.

Scared is the first thought that comes to mind. Am I ready to be a father? Well really, when the hell is anyone?

Usually most men are married first, or in a serious relationship, so it's not a complete surprise when they hear they are going to become a father.

But hey, no matter what I might prefer, the scenario is here. And like it or not, I need to figure this shit out.

Can I be a good father? My own dad was a bastard. I've got a good road map on what *not* to do based on what he was like.

Vinnie surprised me when he left. After the smack down he gave about being self-centered in most of my relationships, he reassured me that he and Gino would be here, as brothers and uncles, to help me with the baby. His generosity and support triggered my current ruminations.

Would I have offered the same? I shake my head, still unhappy when I recall my immediate answer—it was one that left me ashamed. Perhaps a part of me has some hidden resentment at helping to support them and our mom in the early years. The mere idea of one of them having a child now—one I would be expected to help out with—had anger boiling under my skin. It felt awful. It feels crappy to admit it now, even if only to myself.

I can't control Portia's actions, or even her motivations for that matter. But I can control how I react to them. I need to hold my head up high, like Heather does so often when she's afraid, and handle the possibility of a baby with the way I handle business—with professionalism, respect, and an eye on the big picture. In this case, it's not a high revenue merger, but the chance to share my life with someone, in this case a child, and help them grow into a better person than I am.

When you put it all into perspective, I really have been an ass.

Chapter Fifteen

Heather

The train ride to Philly was kind of relaxing. No one sat near me in the business car, a miracle on its own, and then no one bothered me to plug in their laptop or phone while I worked at a table in the dining car. It was exactly what I needed—peace and quiet. Especially after over-imbibing last night with Carla.

The longer I think about Tony's reaction to Portia being pregnant, the more disturbed I become. I keep replaying his words over and over in my mind. At the end, after he revealed his staggering net worth, he *almost* seemed close to pulling his head out of his ass. But not quite.

Is it my role in our relationship to help him *not* be such a jerk regarding the possible pregnancy? Or is it an indicator that no matter how drawn I am to him sexually that maybe he's not ready for a real relationship, one that requires responsibility and commitment?

Can I be content with staying with him even while I'm worried I may be another fling he eventually tires of? Then again, is there any genuine guarantee in any relationship? My folks were happy together for over twenty years. If they hadn't died in the car crash, I'd assume they would have been one of the couples who truly made it for the long haul—the one all the way to the golden years. They weren't like other empty-nesters I'd seen—like my college friends' parents—where the marriage falls apart when the kids left home.

Their lives didn't revolve around me, an accomplishment in itself considering I was an only child. Watching them relate to one another and thrive over the years made me yearn to find such happiness for myself. Maybe that's why I've had a tendency to jump feet first into a relationship without looking. Always hoping the next guy, the next relationship, would be my very own happily ever after.

And yet, here I stand now... dating a guy who might very well be a "baby daddy," a term which makes me shudder, for another woman. Albeit, a very rich and successful baby daddy, but an unmarried father just the same. How do we as a society look at such men? Do we revile them as irresponsible, commitment-phobes who knock up any woman dumb enough to fall for their promises of undying love... or could some of the men be victims of circumstance too? I'll admit, I never really wasted too many brain cells on thinking about the guy;

my outrage has always been for the perceived jilted woman left to raise a child on her own.

While I'm not as ready as Tony to paint a woman, one who I've never met, as manipulative and a gold digger, I'm not so naive to think women like that don't exist. We can be predators just as easily as any guy.

All I know is, no matter how drawn I am to Tony, we can't let things lie as they are. I don't think I could spend my life with someone who reviled their child's mother simply because of an accidental conception. Assuming, of course, Tony and I were even cut out for a long term relationship.

A sigh escapes me as I gather my things and prepare to disembark. I really want to drown my sorrows and confusion in a bottle of wine, but judging by the success of last night, it obviously won't help.

I take a cab to my hotel and check in. In a few minutes, I'm settled in my room with the whole night ahead of me. I run a hot bath and pour shampoo from the tiny bottles on the vanity under the running water. Bubbles foam and a light citrusy scent fills the air. I strip, then grab my cell and eReader and climb into the half-full tub.

The heat sinks into my muscles, bringing a soothing relaxed feel to wash away the day. I debate on calling Tony now or after I get out of the tub. I know I'm procrastinating, but damn, this stuff isn't easy. Deep in my heart, I know I'm not going to end things with him over his behavior with Portia. It would be too premature of me, especially when we may find out the baby isn't his.

I still have faith in him and us. We could work out to be long term if we can work through this—and I know we can. It's coming to terms with all the changes so quickly that has set me off my game.

My phone *bings* softly on the side of the tub, indicating a text has come in. It's Tony.

Hey— did you get in okay? Haven't heard from you.

A long sigh eases out of me as I realize I've got to face him, even if it's only figuratively as we're not in person.

I dry off my hand before picking up the phone, and decide to call him back rather than text. He picks up on the first ring.

"Hi," he says. "I take it you're at the hotel?"

"Yes. Soaking in the tub. I was planning on calling when I was done."

"Uh-huh, sure. You couldn't possibly be avoiding me after I dropped two major bombs on you yesterday?"

He's more observant than I give him credit for. "Maybe." I smile. "Maybe not. It was really the one thing —the possibility of you becoming a father—that's stayed with me. Your money never mattered to me."

"Hmmm…"

We're both quiet for a couple of breaths. I'd almost call it a pregnant silence, but if I did that I'd probably crack up laughing. A little snort of awkwardness escapes me.

"What's that?" Tony asks. "Did you say something?"

"No. I was kind of hoping you would."

"I… I don't know what to say. It seems like too much to cover on the phone."

"Yeah, I know what you mean." I close my eyes and push out what I'm feeling, ignoring the icy pit in my stomach. "You kind of came across as an insensitive jerk yesterday."

Tony lets out a long sigh on the other end of the line. "You're being kind. I was a bit of a dick. With my head up my ass."

An inappropriate chuckle bubbles out. "That's an interesting picture you're painting with your words. Kind of uncomfortable sounding, too."

Tony returns my humor, cutting short his own awkward laugh. "I never said I was great with words. Sorry."

"You seem to do all right for yourself when it really matters."

"I'm not so sure I agree. You really matter to me and I seem to be sticking my foot in my mouth lately—and right when it counts."

My heart lurches in my chest. Do I respond to his declaration or let it lie? I go for it. Yay me. "So... I really matter to you, huh?"

"Yes. You do." He sighs again and I picture him snuggling into one of the big comfy couches in his living room. "Have I not been clear on how I feel?"

"Have either of us, Tony?" I smile. This call must be just as hard for him as it is for me. "I mean, sometimes we talk, sometimes we're too *busy* to talk, you know?"

A satisfied sound of humor reaches me. "Yeah, you're right." Then more silence. "Okay, I'm just going to say it.

I'm falling for you, Heather. Despite only knowing you for a month. And... I'm..."

My heart feels like it wants to climb up my throat. I'm so shocked and happy I can't find any words. I stutter out a meek, "Y-y-yes?"

"Damn. This talking about how you feel shit is hard. How do you ladies do it?"

I laugh, some of the tension easing out of me. No matter how awkward I'm feeling, this is Tony. The man who strung himself up with chains for me to take pictures. I know him. He's not Jimmy, he's not Rick. He's my Tony.

"We muddle through, pretending we know what we're talking about most of the time," I say.

"Ah, so that's the trick."

I swish my toes in the hot water, disrupting bubbles. "Well, we do talk to each other more than guys do, normally. But it's not like I hang out with enough men to really do a comparison."

"Uh-huh."

I circle him back, hoping he will reveal whatever it was he was about to say. "You were about to say something before. Started with an *and*."

"And what?"

"Uh..." I backpedal, the courage draining right out of me. "Never mind."

"You caught that, huh? And now you want me to say what I was trying to get out before."

"Only if you want to."

"Jesus," I picture him running a hand through his hair as he often does when frustrated. "Okay, this is hard." He pauses. "I'm kind of scared."

My skin tightens. Electric tingles make the hair on my arm stand on end. "Scared of what?"

"Of losing you over this whole mess with Portia. I... I don't know what to do. And I know I've been an ass."

"Oh, Tony." I overcome my own fear to reassure him. "I'm falling for you, too. And I know exactly what you mean about being scared."

"So what do we do?"

"I'm thinking we'll need to talk out this whole baby situation face to face, rather than on the phone." I hesitate once more, then boldly say what's on my mind. "But really, the big deal stuff will be on your end."

"Mine?"

"You need to figure out what you want regarding this child, and you need to do that on your own. It's not something I can do for you."

"My brother Vinnie already read me the riot act. It's a lot to come to terms with."

"Yes, it is."

"Will you stay with me throughout it all?"

I consider his question carefully. I can't say yes without knowing what he plans to do. "That depends on you and how you decide to handle it. Attitude is everything."

"Fair enough. Let's talk more tomorrow night, okay?"

"Okay."

There's a moment of silence, and then Tony says, "How was your day?"

"Not bad. Still getting the lay of the land at work."

"Getting along well with Tammy? How's she working out?"

I think about her dating Jimmy and push the thoughts away. She's an adult. She can make up her own mind. That will become my new mantra until it sticks. "Great so far. If I need someone permanent, she's a good fit."

We're quiet again and I wonder if I should make an excuse and get off the phone. But a part of me refuses, enjoying the time talking to him even if nothing important is said.

"What did you do today?" I ask.

"Worked on the dry wall in my new office. It's coming along nicely."

"Can't wait to see it." And interestingly enough, I mean every word. I love seeing the progress he makes each day. Much more tangible than working with spreadsheets and emails, like me.

"Maybe we can christen the new room with another indoor picnic," he says, a hint of naughty in his voice.

"I like the sound of that."

"I like the sound of your voice."

"You do?" I lower my voice, aiming for sexy. "And I wasn't even trying."

"Oh... but you sound like you are now."

"Maybe." The warm water feels good on my skin. And teasing him a little has helped me to relax.

"So... are you still in the tub?"

"Yes."

"Are there bubbles?"

I laugh. "Yes, there are."

A soft groan of appreciation spills from him. "That sounds really... nice..."

I hear the rasp of a zipper. "Did you just unzip your fly?"

"Maybe."

And just like that, heat floods my middle, warming it more than the hot water already has. "You're a naughty boy, aren't you?"

"That depends. Will my being naughty get me time with the ping pong paddle again? Because if the answer is yes, then I'm definitely being naughty."

"Mmmm... it just might." Feeling bold and daring I ask, "What are you wearing and where are you?"

"I'm sitting up on my bed, wearing jeans and a tee shirt."

"Nice." My free hand drifts under the water, where I lightly stroke the top of my mound, testing if I'm really game to push this little scenario to the hilt. My eyes drift closed as I listen to his increased breathing. Arousal brews inside, indicating that yes, I sure as hell can be the type of girl who engages in phone sex. I stifle a low moan, unwilling to reveal myself yet.

"What are you doing in the tub?"

"Just soaking. Naked."

He chuckles, low and sexy. "How else would you be in the tub?"

I slip my fingers down to tease my outer folds. "Touché." I strengthen my tone, knowing he likes it when I take control. "Take out your cock."

"Damn. You're serious, huh?"

"Do it," I command.

"Yes, ma'am." His breathing changes and I hear a rustle of clothing.

"Are you stroking it?" I ask as my fingers delve deeper, slipping down to my opening.

"Yes."

"Is it growing nice and hard in your hand?"

"Oh God." His breath pushes out. "It certainly is."

I pump a slim finger inside, noting the slick feel not attributed to water. "Tell me what you like. Tell me what you think is sexy."

His voice comes across the phone low and intense. "I love seeing you in high heels. I picture bending you over whenever you're wearing them, and taking you hard and fast."

The heel of my hand presses against my clit, rubbing slow and hard as I thrust a second finger into my depths. My voice sounds low and breathy, quite sexy in the acoustics of the steamy bathroom. "Ohh... that sounds too good to resist. It's going to be the first thing I think of now when I wear heels around you."

"I love fisting that long hair of yours in my hand and holding on too tight. It's like I'm claiming you while I'm fucking you."

Tony doesn't normally swear much, but in this moment, it drives me to the brink, imagining he's right there with me.

Unable to hold off any longer, I remove my fingers and focus on my tiny clit. "God, that's sexy as hell. I'm going to come soon, Tony."

"Are you? Are you touching yourself under all those bubbles, Heather?"

"Yes, I am."

"Are you sliding those slim fingers back and forth over that little wet clit, teasing it while you think of me pulling your hair and fucking you hard?"

I moan into the phone. "Oh, yes. That's right."

His own breathing becomes rough, caressing my ear through the cell phone. "I'm stroking my cock for you. Thinking about those thigh-high black boots with the long silver zipper down the back. You looked so hot in those."

"I love watching you come, Heather. The little smile on your face. The crash of pleasure over your features. The sounds you make when you're lost in the moment."

I don't respond, too caught up in playing with my clit. I'm right there. Ready to fly over the edge.

"You know what I love the most?" he asks, his voice hoarse with desire. "I love that I'm the one who made you feel that way."

I groan again, circling my hips under the bubbles, racing toward my finish.

"Come for me, baby. I want to hear you."

My orgasm swells inside, drawing out languidly with my moans.

"Oh, that's it. I hear you." Tony's breathing turns ragged and rough while I slowly climb toward my peak.

The proverbial dam breaks inside and pleasure washes through me, weakening my limbs, making me grateful I'm in the tub. Unlike most of the time when I masturbate, this release continues, longer and sweeter, like the pleasure I receive when I'm with Tony.

My whimpers and moans of ecstasy set Tony off on the other end of the line and I hear him reach his climax as well. His orgasm sounds loud and sexy as hell, making me wish I was there to see what it does to him.

There's a comfortable silence between us as we both come down from our high.

It's not lost on me how many times Tony used the word "love" to describe how he felt. For the first time in my life, possible baby or not, I feel like everything may work out for me in a relationship. And it makes my heart swell with emotion.

Chapter Sixteen

Tony

Last night seemed like a turning point for Heather and me. We still have a lot to sort out, but it feels like we're on solid ground and that's all that matters. I know I've fallen for her—hard. How could I not when she's so amazing?

You sound like a love-struck teenager. Going to carve your initials in a tree next?

Whatever. I don't need to analyze it. Waste of time. Just accept and enjoy.

I want her to meet my family. But it wouldn't be right to introduce her to everyone *and* not tell my mom about the possible baby. She'd flip. I'm still coming to terms with all of it—but I don't need DNA proof to finally grow up and face my responsibilities like a man. It might burn my gut to tell my mom, but it's the right thing to do.

It's doing the right thing that matters in life, even if it's difficult. Hell, the easy way out is called the "easy way" for a reason—because it's not hard. And when have I ever backed down from a challenge?

Thoughts of impending fatherhood roll over and over in my mind as I scroll through the pictures Heather uploaded to the computer from her new camera. There are some remarkable ones of the building and my roof top garden. What would it be like to share all the things I've helped build with a child? Would I see the world anew through the wonder in his or her eyes?

I pause over a particular favorite of mine and send it to the commercial printer sitting next to me, opting for an eleven by seventeen print size. This one will proudly hang in my new home office. Maybe I should be contemplating a room for a baby, too.

Hold on now. A baby in my bachelor pad. Let's not put the cart before the horse. That's a curve ball I hadn't intended. But then again, who plans for an unexpected surprise like this when they always had protected sex?

And then there's Portia's demands to consider. After paternity testing we'd have to discuss custody. What if she has no plans to share custody? I bet money would change her mind. Am I ready to tackle the responsibility of having a baby even part of the time? Would my mother want to help or be resentful I asked?

She's been having a good time traveling with her church group and dating again. May have taken her a decade of therapy but she's finally ready and I'm glad. Gino and Vinnie still seem a little on the fence, almost as if they're afraid of losing our mom to another man. She's in her early fifties. I'd rather see her happy and carefree than anything else in the world.

Maybe I'd need to hire help with a baby. Panic sends a shiver of sweat down my spine. I've never even changed a diaper. Holy shit, what has my perfectly ordered life become?

One minute I'm on my knees, receiving orders from the sexiest woman I've ever met in my life, and the next I'm getting doused with a cement truck full of cold water —told I may be the father of a child with a frivolous socialite. Talk about life changing. And slightly depressing.

I shove the complicated thoughts away, determined to address them later, when I have more time to ruminate over the bigger picture.

Assuming the baby is yours.

Yeah, only need to wait twelve more weeks to find out. No pressure.

In a few minutes, I scroll from the building shots to the ones of our sexy shoot last week, and all thoughts of children and future possibilities flee my mind. Heather's expertise in the medium shines in these pictures. The light and shadows playing over my skin look dangerous, like I could be a professional model and these are shots for a new brand of distressed jeans. Although, the chains lend a distinct BDSM feel to the setting. Might not be what an advertiser would want. Then again, what the hell do I know?

Still, my eyes keep lingering over the images. They're provocative and evoke a sense of sensuality. Hmm... maybe if I crop some of these to take my face out.

Over the next hour I darken and lighten shadows, play with cropping and scale, then print the ones I think look the best. Laying them on the flat surfaces of the studio, I have to say I'm impressed. There are some serious art quality shots here. I carry a few into the living room when I run out of table space in the studio.

There's a pounding at my door, which is unexpected as I don't have any deliveries scheduled for today. I head toward the door, hearing my brothers familiar voices as I reach the hall past the kitchen.

I open the door to see I was right, both boneheads decided to stop in unannounced. "And to what do I owe this unexpected visit?"

Vinnie pushes in first, a determined look on his face, followed closely by the youngest, Gino. Seeing them both side by side, you'd never think they were brothers—me and Gino, no doubt. But Vinnie, or as he prefers to be called, Vince, inherited some blond gene that must have been recessive. If he hadn't looked so much like our dad in facial features I'm sure there would have been hell to pay for my poor mom.

Unlike Gino and me, who look Italian through and through, Vinnie has light blue eyes and sandy blond hair. He and my friend Marcus look more like brothers than we do.

Vinnie stares at me, unflinching. "I told him."

"Told him what?" I ask, a vague sense of unease settling in my gut.

"About Portia."

Gino shoves my shoulder. "You couldn't tell me yourself, you fucking coward?"

Anger pushes to the forefront of my mind. "You son of a bitch." I glare at Vinnie. "You had to open your mouth. Like some damn gossiping yenta." A fist closes over my heart. "You didn't tell Mom did you?" Unconsciously my hand curls into a fist as well. "I think I might have to kill you if you did."

Vinnie shakes his head no and advances deeper into my apartment. I follow and my little brother pushes my back once more. "Seriously? Is that all you have to say? Weren't you the one always preaching shit to us growing up like 'no glove, no love'?"

My other brother chimes in from the kitchen, "Or my personal favorite, 'Wrap it before you tap it.'"

"Or the one you shouted when I left to pick up my prom date," Gino says. "'Cloak that joker, before you poke her.'"

Laughter bubbles up as we follow him down the hall, effectively diffusing my anger, with the memories the two bring up.

"Not as bad as my first date with Jennifer James, damn she was smokin' hot. 'Don't be a fool, cover your tool.'"

Tears start to leak out of my eyes, I'm laughing so hard. "All right, you sorry bastards. I get it! Stop already.

And for your information, I *was* protected." I shrug. "I'm not sure how it happened."

Gino shoves his hands in his pocket. "Vinnie said it might not be yours. Is that the truth?"

"I have no idea, man. I don't know this girl all that well."

Vinnie looks around, notices a print and walks toward it. "You knew her well enough to screw her... repeatedly."

He's standing over one Heather took of the plants on my roof-top garden. There's a spectacular view of the skyline in the background. It's a nice contrast of the lush greenery transposed over the industrialized progress.

"Sex isn't a big deal to some women," I say. "And she was one of them. She liked to have fun. Liked to party. We had some good times together, went to a few society functions. Really, it wasn't a major time investment from either of us."

Gino starts in again, "And now you might pay the ultimate price for the next eighteen to twenty two years." A wry grimace twists his face. "Doesn't seem fair when you've been careful all your life."

Vinnie smile. "Yeah, especially when considering the extraordinary humiliation you put us through with your little 'helpful' sayings."

For the first time since I found out Portia was pregnant, I'm not pissed off. Nor am I thinking the worst case scenario that she's a money grubbing gold digger out for my millions. I bet Heather would be proud of me. Yup. I'd call that personal growth.

"You know what, assholes? It is what it is. No sense wasting my time complaining and angling to get out of it. We'll just have to see what the test results say."

"Wow," my youngest brother says. "You're taking it much better than I thought." He wanders over to see what Vinnie is admiring. "Hey, where did these come from? Are they of this building?"

"Yeah, Tony," Vinnie says. "These are really good."

"Thanks. Heather took them. I'll tell her you like them, she'll be pleased."

"These are like, professional good." Gino says, picking one up by the edges for a closer look. "Do you have any more?"

"Yeah, come on back. I'll show you."

They both saw the studio Sunday, neither one commented on it then, more eager to get to the game than admire my hard work.

"Huh," Vinnie says, trailing slowly after me. "I wondered what or who you made the studio for. Should have guessed. But honestly, how could I have known? You've never done anything like this for a woman before."

My heart swells with pride as the two knuckleheads walk around the room and look at all the pictures, even the provocative ones of me.

Gino lets out a low whistle. "Damn, don't know if you want Mom to see these or not."

Before I answer, Vinnie chimes in. "Are you kidding? She'll love it. So proud of her first born. She'll probably share them with her church friends."

"There's a thought that gives me the creeps," Gino says. "Thanks."

Vinnie hovers over one and points. "Um, maybe not this one. Dude, are you hard?"

I laugh, uncaring what the two think as long as Heather is happy. "Yeah, man. That happens when the photographer starts to strip. Go figure."

Vinnie stares at me and nods. "You sound happy, man. I'm glad. You deserve it." I nod back, acknowledging his sentiment. "Bring her to dinner on Sunday. Surprise Mom. She'll be ecstatic."

"What about the baby issue? Can I really introduce Mom to a girl with a possible paternity issue hanging over me?"

"Don't tell her," he says. "You can't say anything until you know for sure. The storm of drama you'd open up would be unreal. Much better to have her meet Heather and save the other 'til you have proof."

I nod. "You're right. I'll ask Heather over for dinner. Mom will love meeting her."

They look at the rest of the pictures, commenting more on the scenery and building shots than the others.

"They're impressive, man," Vinnie says. "She's got talent."

"Good thing your face is cut out of these." Gino is examining one of me on the chaise. "Not that it sounds like you care either way. Did you print these for a showing?"

"As in a gallery?" I respond. Now that he says it, I realize it's a great idea. "I hadn't thought of that."

Vinnie adds his opinion. "Yeah, they are definitely artsy enough for a gallery." He snorts. "Assuming the place will show half-naked, aroused men."

"You guys gave me a great idea. I think I'll call an old friend later. Now did the two of you come over for any reason other than to bust my balls over the baby? Don't you guys have jobs?"

"We came specifically to harass you. Now that you're unemployed and all." Gino just smiles. "That's the joy and curse of retail. Mornings off, work late."

Vinnie picks up a print of a bridge leading into New York. "I'm on my way into the restaurant from here. Hey, can I take this one for the bar? The black and white is really classy."

"I need to ask Heather first." Impulsively I grab a large envelope and slip it in. "You know what? I don't think she'll mind. Take it and if she says no I'll call you to take it down. Sound good?" I'm eager to push the two out the door so I can make a few phone calls and print more shots.

It takes another twenty minutes or so, but soon I'm alone again. I grab my cell and call the friend I mentioned, the one who owns a small gallery in midtown.

As luck would have it, the gallery isn't showing anyone this weekend. Something about a botched delivery and a last minute cancellation. My friend wants to see what I've got, so I email a few dozen pics.

Immediately I get a call back to messenger over forty of the best pictures from the files on hand. He'd like to have them framed and up for a preview for the other gallery owners tomorrow. If things work out like I hope, this could be the best surprise I've planned for Heather yet.

Chapter Seventeen

Heather

"Hey, Heather," Jimmy calls from my office doorway.

It's late in the day and now I regret stopping here after catching an earlier train back from Philly. Should have just gone straight home. Idiot.

"Hi, Jimmy. What do you want?"

He tsks at me while stepping into my office. "Now that's no way to talk to a man. You should try for amiable and polite."

And you should fuck off and die. I somehow restrain the words busting to spew out. "I don't have time for your games. Do you need something or not?"

He grins, small and secretive, before glancing over his shoulder quickly. "I think I *need* you back on your knees, Heather. That always was your best position."

Fear lances through me at his boldness. Who says such shit at work? "Geez, cut it out, Jimmy. I've got no qualms about reporting your ass to HR for harassment."

He backs away, hands raised in a placating gesture. "Just kidding, doll face. Since when did you lose your sense of humor?"

"Right when you started working here. What gives? Why did you take the job anyway?"

He shrugs and steps back. "When life offers me a challenge, I take it."

What a prick. At my stare he leaves, obviously he wasn't here for any other reason than to rile me up.

A little while later, right before quitting time, squeals of delight come from the cubicles in front of my office door. Hoping I didn't mess up and miss contributing for someone's birthday cake in the office, I poke my head out to investigate. A huge bouquet sits on Tammy's desk, and she's grinning ear from ear.

Dread settles in my stomach. Jimmy did the exact same thing with me. A dinner, then flowers, all strategically done as a weekend approaches. More than likely he's going to ask her out tomorrow or Friday for drinks and then the rest will be history.

I hesitate, unsure if I should say anything, especially here and now in the middle of her happiness, in front of the whole office. God, I'm a wimp for not saying anything sooner. I glance up and see Jimmy watching me from across the office. There's a cold and calculating expression darkening his face. What I wouldn't give for Tammy to turn and see it all on her own.

But no. She's too busy sniffing the roses and grinning while she re-reads the card over and over again.

Anger and frustration boils up and over, propelling me down the hall, no direction in mind. I need to get this *crap* out of my system. What I also need, is to let sleeping dogs lie and leave his shit behind me. She's a grown woman, she's free to make her own mistakes.

Footsteps sound behind me as I approach one of the empty conference rooms. "Jealous?" Jimmy's voice rasps softly. A strong hand wraps around my elbow as he steps up beside me. I glance up as I'm propelled toward the open door, to see an unsmiling Jimmy escorting me inside.

I jerk my arm out of his hold and slam on the lights. Fear bubbles below the surface as I see him shut the door behind us, until I realize shapes of our co-workers are visible through the frosted glass next to the doors. I'm safe. I can scream if he tries anything. "What the hell are you talking about? Of course I'm not jealous."

A confidant, cocky smile rests on his smug face. "Really? You sure as hell looked like you were a moment ago."

"You're delusional. That was anger at myself you saw —over my indecision. Whether or not I should say anything to Tammy about you."

"And what would you say?" He steps closer, reaching out to touch me, but drawing back at the last moment. "Do you want *everyone* to know we dated and you were bad in bed?"

"God no. That would be hell. Maybe I'll tell everyone you're a womanizing bastard. That might put a crimp in your style."

"And who would believe you? I'd make sure you looked like a jealous ex now that everyone knows I'm dating your assistant." His look turns calculating, like he's taking my measure. "Or maybe you'd go another route, and tell Tammy how I pushed you to your knees? Or how much you enjoyed choking on my cock?"

My eyes dart nervously to the door. I reach out and grasp the handle, not liking where this conversation is going. "Why would I tell anyone that? I never liked when you insisted and got forceful. Who the hell would?"

He shrugs, seeming not to notice how tense I am or that I'm about to bolt back into the hall. "You'd be surprised what some ladies like. You didn't complain at the time."

"There's a lot I didn't know back then. I've grown a lot. Changed. Realized I don't need to be a doormat to keep a man."

A dark look crosses his face. "You have changed, Heather. Finally grew a back bone."

Deciding I've had enough from him, I open the door, my heart racing in my chest. His voice trails after me as I escape, "As long as you keep your mouth shut we won't have any problems."

What the hell is that supposed to mean? Does he think this is some game we're playing? I stomp down the hall, fear and anger mixing for dominance in my body. Good God, he's freakin' crazy. The best thing I can do is avoid him. And not engage in future conversations, obviously.

Should I say anything to my bosses? What proof do I have? Is it sexual harassment when I just feel harassed? Then again, the shit he said about getting me on my knees should definitely qualify for sexual harassment.

I scamper back to my office and close the door before sinking into the chair behind my desk. Sweat trickles down my back, plastering the fabric of my blouse to my spine, leaving a sticky unclean feeling behind. I take a few deep breaths to calm my heart. This is ridiculous. I'm a grown woman. I *can* handle a slime ball like him.

How? How do you intend to keep the upper hand with a creep like that?

What the hell should I do? Maybe if he tries something again I could record him.

Yeah, that'll work. Because all you'd have to do is casually ask him to wait while you unobtrusively set your cell phone to record. Idiot.

The only way such a plan would work is if I turned on my cell ahead of time and deliberately set out to put myself in a situation where he could approach me and spew some of his craziness. Which sounds really unsafe. Not to mention dangerous. Like out of a kidnap-and-kill type of movie scenario.

I can't believe I ever slept with such an asshole. Was I that desperate? Or was it more that it all happened so slowly? I never noticed the cruel edge to him when we had sex, the desperation, not until I felt uncomfortable with his pressure and stopped enjoying what we were doing. That's about the time when the texting and late night phone calls started—maybe two months into our relationship.

By the time I caught him cheating, I had lost all sense of self. If I'm honest, I was a shadow of a woman. I think about the give and take of power in what I have with Tony. Sure, we may be hitting a rough patch right now, but I still don't feel like he's trying to dominate me or make me submit to his will, like Jimmy did.

Does Jimmy think the way he treats women is normal and acceptable? Have too many women read BDSM erotic romance books and fantasized about a dominant man who takes what he wants when he wants, *no matter what*? Could such a woman become caught up in the sexual moment and be unaware of what's really going on in the creep's head until it's too late? Is that, in a way, what happened to me? Did I want love so badly I was willing to be treated poorly to get it?

I lean my head down on the edge of my desk, on crossed arms, and stare at the carpet. Thinking about what I went through at the end with Jimmy makes me nauseous. I pull in a deep breath, hoping to calm the queasiness.

Love is about equality, not about one person loving more than the other or the stronger bending the weaker to their will. Sure, there's the weird times we've all experienced in relationships—the awkward beginnings, or when we're all afraid to be the first to declare our feelings, and then there's the uncertainty of perhaps loving someone who doesn't love you back... but that's more *new* relationship stuff.

With time spent should come trust. Trust I thought I had with Jimmy, but was too stupid to realize was simply him controlling me. Ready to shake off the poison from my encounter with the bastard, I rise and stretch, tensing and releasing my muscles one by one. I need to get him out of my head.

I am in a healthy relationship. Tony and I may play with spanking and tying each other up, or even with ordering the other around sexually, but it's never about dominating and all about sexual exploration—something that can only be done with someone you trust. I am with a man who wants me for me, not one who wants to own me. There is a difference and I feel sorry for the women in bad relationships who can't tell what's healthy and what isn't.

Should I call Carla? Even though we clashed a bit when Tony and I first started dating, she's been a good friend for years and always tries to help with advice. She was there for me when it counted with Jimmy, too.

Okay, none of this rambling has helped me make a decision. Free of the urge to vomit I can suddenly think clearer. A decision that's obvious—and right in front of me—and *very* hard to do. One I can practically hear Carla screaming in my mind.

I need to do what so many women are afraid of. I have to go to the Human Resources department and lay everything on the line. I check the clock; it's quarter to five. They probably won't appreciate me dumping something this heavy on them at the end of the day, but I've got to do it. Before I back out and second guess myself as I've done before when a situation is difficult.

I straighten my spine and take a deep breath. Fear bubbles in my gut, tightens my stomach muscles, and makes me shake. I can do this. I walk out of my office, head held high, and make my way to HR.

I knock on Mrs. Stephenson's door and she waves me in with a welcoming smile.

By the time I'm done spilling my guts, I feel strangely empowered and absolved of guilt. A few times in the beginning I almost cried, but I forced the tears down and stuck to the facts. The result was like a weight being lifted from my shoulders.

It had to be done. The company paid out thousands to settle two very bad sexual harassment suits a few weeks ago with two other salesmen no longer with the company. I heard slimy details that implied what the four women went through was much worse than what I've experienced. Mrs. Stephenson assured me if those ladies had come to her earlier, things never would have gotten as bad as they did, resulting in therapy and law suits.

It's after six when I leave her office and I'm glad she didn't mind staying to hear me out and take down all my concerns. Heads will roll tomorrow, figuratively if not literally, starting with a long talk with Jimmy's boss. I don't know if my ex will lose his job, and frankly, I don't care.

That bastard deserves everything he gets.

Smiling, feeling better than I have all week, I call Tony.

He answers right away. "Where are you?" I ask, my voice low and sexy.

"I'm at your place. Got here thirty minutes ago, hoping to meet you from Philly. What happened?"

"Got held up at work, but I'm all yours now. And—I have plans."

"Do you, now?" I hear the interest in his voice. "I'm intrigued."

"I'd prefer you naked. I'll be home in fifteen minutes."

He chuckles, a hint of confidence and anticipation in the sound, "Yes, ma'am."

Chapter Eighteen

Tony

For the first time in my life, I'm actually looking forward to *talking* to a woman. And I don't mean casual conversation, either. That's always easy. Or dirty talk. Also easy.

I mean like one of those times when they sit you down to talk to you like you're insensitive, or stupid. Yeah, like that. Only this time it's good. About this whole baby thing. About how shitty I acted in the beginning... all of it. And hopefully she'll find it somewhere in her heart to hear me out.

I'm not averse to begging if I have to. Although, we did end things well on the phone last night so that might not be an issue.

Heather bursts through the front door, full of energy. The gleam in her eye looks faintly animalistic. I grin in anticipation. Looks like someone got themselves worked up into a sexy tizzy on the way home. My cock stirs in my pants at the mere thought. Down boy. She may want to talk first.

"Go to the bedroom and take off your clothes."

"So, we'll talk later?"

She grabs my face and kisses me, hard. "Later would be best. Do you mind?"

"Hell no."

"Good." She smacks my ass, a brazen smile on her face. "Go do as you're told."

I smile, uncaring that our talk will happen later rather than sooner. "Yes, ma'am." She wants to play first, who am I to complain? In my mind, it re-enforces we're going to work things out. She wouldn't be raring to tear off my clothes if she was mad enough to end things with me.

I stride down the hall, doing my best to rein in my own eagerness so she doesn't laugh at me. In a flash, I strip off my clothes and dive onto the big bed. My burgeoning erection strains toward my belly, growing harder by the second.

Heather struts, there's no other word for it, toward me, working her hips for all she's got. "I did it," she says casually, while detouring toward her dresser.

"Good for you," I say enthusiastically. I pat the bed sheet beside me. "Come join me."

She laughs, the sound full of confidence and promise. "Don't you even want to know *what* I did?"

"Sure. Go ahead."

Heather reaches into a drawer and removes several silk scarves and a vibrator. Hmm... I wonder what she has in mind. She turns back to me with a devilish grin. "Lay down and spread your arms. Place your ankles about a foot apart."

"Uh... Okay." I comply, still not sure where this is going. She'd tell me if she planned on shoving that vibrator into me, right? I'm sure she would.

Slim hands wrap a scarf around my wrist and tie a knot. Next, she reaches past the corner of the mattress and secures the fabric, tying me in place.

"So... what happened at work? You were going to tell me what you did."

"Why yes, my dear man. I *am* going to tell you." She giggles while securing my ankle in the same fashion. "That ex I told you about at work?"

"Uh-huh. Jimmy?"

She nods. "I reported him to Human Resources. Not going to let him make trouble for me at work."

I try to sit up on the bed, hampered partially by the bond on one wrist. "Hold up now. What happened? Why didn't you say anything to me?"

She shrugs and moves on to my other ankle. "It wasn't anything concrete I could put my finger on until today. Just a creepy feeling whenever he was near. But late this afternoon at work, he crossed a line. And I resisted the desire to run away, thanks in part to you, and shoved him back to the other side."

"Uh... okay. What is an appropriate response from me? I think I need to kick this guy's ass."

One hot hand trails up my calf, to my thigh, lingering near the top, mere inches from my shaft and balls. "And I appreciate that you would. But I needed to handle this on my own." Her fingertips trail lightly across my erect flesh. "Owning my fear and doing something about it felt... incredibly... Empowering." She smiles at me, her expression full of heat and longing. "Which was a very *sexy* feeling."

"I can tell you something else that feels incredible right now."

She chuckles, a low throaty sound that pushes all my buttons. "I just bet you could, big boy." She trails her fingers down my length, and then away, leaving me straining toward her hand for more.

She approaches the head of the bed, that earlier mischief glowing bright. The last scarf drapes loosely from her left hand. "So how 'bout it?" Heather motions to my last free limb. "Are you comfortable with where I want to take this?"

I nod and settle back on the pillows, freely offering her my wrist. "I'm ready for anything you want, darling. As long as you're okay with the work issue."

The silk tightens on my wrist and then my arm stretches out while she secures me. "I'm more than okay." She smacks my bicep lightly. "I am fired up, cowboy."

A low groan escapes me. "You would have to say that. Now I'm picturing those chaps you mentioned the other day."

"We don't have any," she says as she pulls her blouse off. "But we'll have to get some... soon."

I track her every movement, becoming more aroused with each inch of flesh revealed. My cock pulses slowly in place, bobbing to the beat of my pulse. "Damn, Heather. You are unbelievably hot."

She winks at me and finishes undressing, shucking her remaining work clothes into a heap on the floor. "And you would know."

My dark-haired temptress crawls onto the large bed, her long tresses spilling over one pale shoulder to curl on top of her right breast. Her nipples stand at attention, hard and begging to be licked. I moisten my lips in anticipation, hoping she'll come close enough for me to taste.

"I've been dreaming about tying you up, Tony."

"Oh, really? That little taste Saturday night with one of my silk ties was fantastic."

"I know." She scoots close and lies next to me, molding her body to mine. "That's why I couldn't get it out of my head." She leans forward and takes one of my nipples between her lips, sucking hard. The tight skin puckers further under her attention, jolts of pleasure radiating through my chest.

After a few languid pulls, she releases my skin. "I'm so excited I'm not sure I can wait and do all the things I've been dreaming of."

"Like what?"

She slides on top of me, her small breasts pressed to my stomach, her legs straddling my thighs. "I want to ride your face again like I did on the chaise." My cock nudges under her ribs, my hips lifting of their own accord. "I want to spread your thighs and suck your balls 'til you beg me for more." Her hands brace along my sides, and she rises, a seductive smile on her face. "I want to tease your nipples and have you suck mine, too."

I tug on the scarves, desiring to pull her close and kiss her hard. "You can do all those things. And more. I can't stop you."

"*Can't* or *won't*? You know I'll untie those scarves the moment you ask."

"I know. And that's why I won't ask." I stare into her eyes, all the love I'm feeling for her to see. "There's no need to. I trust you. You won't hurt me." I thrust with my hips once more. "Maybe give me blue balls."

Heather laughs, then leans down to gently nip my skin. "Is it really blue balls if you eventually get to come?"

I try to shrug, realize I can't while tied up and say, "Dunno. They're my balls. I can call them blue from extended teasing if I want."

She shifts her weight to one arm, and moves her other hand to cup my balls gently, kneading them slowly in her hand. "Whatever you say. All I know is—I've got you right where I want you."

She stops the kneading and changes to stroking and pulling my sack, gently tugging it from my body.

I clear my throat, suddenly unable to speak clearly. "Oh? And where is that?"

Her dark brown eyes stare into mine. "Right here. In my bed. In my heart." Without another word she leans down and takes my head into her mouth.

Moist heat engulfs the tight skin as a moan rips from my lips. "Oh, Jesus. There's no way I'm going to last."

She slides half way down my shaft and withdraws, leaving me bereft and wishing I'd shut up.

"We can't have that, can we?" She looks up and smiles, her glossy lips stretched wide. "Looks like I'll have to move right to the main event."

I struggle to dig my heels into the mattress so I can push up a bit, but to no avail. I'm not budging thanks to the scarves. "Uh-huh. That might be good."

"What's the matter, Tony?" She teases as she pumps my length. "Afraid you may shoot early?"

I close my eyes against the sensations. "Not if I can help it."

Heather rises again, this time straddling my hips and facing away, giving me an incredible view of her tight little ass. She props one foot on the mattress and the other leg stays bent, her knee planted on the covers. Her long hair cascades down her back, and I fist my hands to control the desire to reach out and grab the silky tresses.

She reaches lower, wraps a hand around me, then positions my head at her entrance. She looks over her shoulder, desire clear on her face. "Have you ever heard of a reverse cowgirl?"

My brain must be firing slower than hers. Is she talking sex positions? I've never bothered to see if they had names. Now I wish I had. "Uh... what?"

She doesn't respond. Instead, she lowers herself slowly onto me. Each inch disappearing little by little, her ass wiggling in tight circles, working me into her heat.

Once I'm seated fully between her thighs she lowers her other knee to the bed, nestling me deeper than I'd thought possible. Her bottom moves, tickling the fine hairs on my lower abdomen. Each subtle brush of flesh emphasizes the tight hold her sheath has on my cock.

"Fucking hell," I gasp out. "That feels incredible."

Just when I think it can't possibly get any better... she rises and rocks down, like she's riding a trotting horse. I tense against the scarves, tightening my biceps, wishing I could wrap my arms around her and thrust up harder and faster.

It's pure torture to lie back and let her take her fill, while every tense inch of me feels driven to rush forward and claim more. To pound hard and speed toward the finish.

Thankfully, my legs are secured near the middle of the bed, so she can bracket my thighs. Smart girl, she must have thought this one out. If I were to widen them so I had enough material to plant my feet, she'd no longer be able to take me like she wants—and we wouldn't want that.

The soft whir of the vibrator sounds and I tense. Where does she plan on sticking that thing? I relax, realizing she can't reach any opening on me or herself in her current position, except for her tiny little clit that likes to play hide and seek.

In a moment, I feel the added stimulation where our bodies meet. It's muted since the vibrations are focused on her flesh and not mine.

"Oh yeah... that's it," she says while touching herself. "Gonna ride you hard."

Considering her mild pulsations back and forth are far from a seriously hard fucking, I can only assume she means figuratively. No sooner does the thought leave my mind and she rises up to place both feet on the mattress, drawing up several inches and then pushing down on my shaft, slamming herself down at the end.

The soft buzzing continues, enticing me to speak. "Are you using that on your clit, Heather?" Before she responds I rush on. "Damn, I bet that's hot. Your sweet little ass is bouncing on my lap... driving me insane." My thighs tighten as sensations wash over me. "I can't take much more."

I test the restraints again, drawing my legs closed as much as possible and thrusting upward to meet her hot, clasping pussy.

Heather leans back, twisting slightly to rest a hand on my chest for leverage while her other one appears locked to her mound. Her legs shake from the strain and I wish my hands were free so I could grip under her thighs and support her.

The tremors slowly work their way through her whole body, until she's one big writhing bundle of pleasure, squirming and pumping up and down as best she can.

Her muscles inside clamp down on me, tiny waves of pressure flexing and releasing deep inside. Loud moans and groans spill from both of us as we race toward completion.

The steady rhythm she established earlier has broken down to frantic coupling. My awkward thrusts upward, me reaching for more contact and a strong need to drive to completion, wars with her circling hips and pistoning body.

The silk knots tighten, cutting off circulation in my hands, but I don't care. All I want is to shoot hard and long inside her. I fist the material in my palm and pull, tense on the edge of my release.

A powerful shout rips from me as my orgasm rushes out. Heather bucks wildly on top, her body convulsing around my cock deep inside her. On and on she comes, milking every drop of strength and come from me in the process.

Gradually, she stills. Her breath bellowing in and out loudly, sweat gleaming on her slender back. She's simply breathtaking in her passion.

"Holy shit," she whispers. "That was powerful."

She drops the vibrator and leans forward to untie my ankles.

I lie back on the pillows and stare at the ceiling. "You aren't kidding."

I feel her moving on the bed, slow and clumsy. "Oh my God, Tony. Your hands! Why didn't you say anything?"

"Huh?" I remember the slight pain. "It was worth it."

She's frantic, trying to untie them, finally running to the kitchen for scissors to cut the fabric.

Very soon, feeling rushes back into them, tingling and biting. I lock in the exclamations dying to burst forth so she doesn't get nervous. Gently she massages my wrists, pulling my arms close to her torso as she rubs.

"I'm so sorry, honey," she says. "I had no idea those knots would tighten."

I sigh, perfectly content and uncaring about the knots or the pain. "It's all right. I'm fine."

"Next time, we'll use cuffs."

I raise an eyebrow and glance at her. "Cuffs?"

She leans in and kisses me. "Not to worry. Not cop handcuffs. I saw these Velcro ones with attachable straps on the website where I got the cock ring and vibrator." She smiles, completely satiated but with a glimmer of more to come. "Bedroom gear. Totally safe. I swear."

I wrap my arms around her and pull her to my chest. "Whatever you want. It's yours."

Chapter Nineteen

Heather

Anything? My mind settles on his last words while love swells inside me. All I want is his heart. Can a girl ask for that? I'm betting it's one of those things you have to wait for. Like Godiva chocolate. It's better when it's given to you as a gift.

I snuggle near the skin between his shoulder and neck, content to breathe in the scent of him. Holy crap that was intense. I tied him up and rode him hard, like I was breaking a stallion.

In a way, isn't that what you're doing? Breaking a wild stallion to the comfort of one mare.

Unsure if that analogy will appeal to a man or insult him, I wisely keep the post-coital babble to myself. I want this moment to last forever. The moment when my heart opened and poured onto my bed. Kind of fitting since this is also where it was broken last.

My stomach growls, pulling me from inner musings that might lead down a darker path.

"Hungry?" Tony asks, his voice a little hoarse, probably from shouting so loudly when he came.

I grin against his skin and kiss him. "For you."

A light smack on my ass startles me, a yip of surprise slipping out. "You trying to kill me, woman?" He laughs. "I need sustenance if I'm expected to perform like that again anytime soon."

I run a hand down his muscled chest and pat his stomach lightly. "Well then, we need to get you some food."

He playfully rolls me over, pinning my hands above my head. "Wasn't it *your* stomach growling?" He leans down and kisses each of my nipples, licking one lightly before moving to the next. "I could feast on you all night." His lips move higher, trailing up my neck as he settles his weight over me. "But this time, I get to tie you up."

My stomach growls again. "If you feed me, I'll do anything you want."

He wiggles his eyebrows and releases my wrists, shoving a hand under my hip to palm one ass cheek. "*Anything?*" His hips snuggle up to mine. "Because there's something I've been interested in trying to this luscious ass of yours."

I grin, happiness coursing through every cell in my body despite his naughty innuendo. "Maybe someday."

Tony shifts to the side so I can get up. "Okay. I can wait for someday."

Within an hour, a pepperoni and sausage pizza has been delivered and we're curled up on the couch, under a pile of blankets. Tony had to answer the door for the delivery guy while I hid in the kitchen, as he refused to let me put on more than a pair of thong underwear.

I love this sexy playful side to him, so I willingly obliged. It felt weird walking around topless, even with the heat turned up, until I noticed Tony watching me. I felt so sexy and desirable from the dark look and naked longing on his face that my awkwardness went away quickly.

After two slices of pizza, and some welcome groping under the covers, Tony says, "Let me start with an apology."

"What for?"

He raises one shoulder, and grabs another slice from the box on the coffee table. "For the obvious—putting us in this situation. Some way, somehow, the condom didn't work. And now here we are, weeks later, with what could be a permanent reminder of my wild life to haunt us forever. I'm sorry to put you through this."

I relax into the comfy couch, content despite the possibility of another woman's baby hanging over us. "Apology accepted—although I'm not sure one was needed. What are *you* going to do? That's the bigger issue."

"I intend to support the child and be a good father. No matter what kind of backward crap the Catholic church might want of its parishioners, I will not marry Portia, even if my mom goes ballistic."

"You're Catholic? Not that it matters to me, but I hadn't thought about how your family might react. Is that why your brother gave you such a hard time the other day?"

"Might have been part of it, but in all honesty, I haven't been to church since before my dad died, and neither have my brothers. Don't think we can be called Catholics anymore—I know I don't consider myself one, but I can't speak for Gino and Vinnie. My mom went all the time, even after he died—maybe the church and her supportive sisters helped her deal with everything. I dunno. It's not like we talked about it a lot. But a part of me resents that the church may also have been what kept her by my deadbeat father's side all those years, too."

"I'm so sorry, Tony. This *situation* is going to get much harder for you before it gets easier."

He leans across the couch and kisses me. "It is what it is. I can't carry anger all the time regarding Portia. It's not healthy." He flops back onto the cushion, his face losing some of his previous good humor.

"Did you ever think that maybe your behavior with dating lots of women was to avoid becoming like your father? The same way you worked hard to prove you were better than him."

"I don't follow."

"Well, if you didn't fall in love and get married... then there was no risk of ever becoming like he was with your mom and your brothers."

Tony looks at me, the intensity in his gaze drilling deep. "Holy shit. I think you're right. I never wanted to be like him, so I avoided serious relationships at all costs—even at my own expense."

I squeeze his hand, thrilled he's made the connection. It bodes well for us having a future together.

"And here I thought I had my shit together all these years. Boy, was I wrong. Rich playboy is actually afraid of falling in love and turning into his loser dad. Nice."

"Oh, come on. Don't you think you're being hard on yourself? You'd be a great dad."

"You really think so?"

"I know so. Look at all you've done since I've met you. You figured out what really made you happy and earning buckets of money was no longer it. You quit the safe corporate job and did what you wanted. Not many of us can say that."

"My top floor in Hoboken does have plenty of space..." Tony begins, sincerity in his eyes. "You know, for a baby room and stuff."

My heart trips in my chest. I'm so impressed with this man. Handed a crappy circumstance and he's come to terms with it. Wow. Even to the extent of making his bachelor pad welcome for a child.

If I was a man in his position, how would I have reacted? I'm not sure, but never the less, he's doing the right thing, which is commendable.

At my silence his voice becomes agitated. "Is that going to be a problem? Will you end things between us if the baby does turn out to be mine? The way we were talking... I just assumed..."

How can I tell him he's already captured my heart? That I'd stand by his side even through a public lynching? Unsure of the words to ease his mind, I reach out and grab his hand under the blanket. "It won't be a problem, Tony. Not to worry. Let's take things one step at a time."

A deep sigh eases out of him. "For a moment there, I thought you'd go running for the hills."

I laugh. God, he has no idea what a catch he is, baby or not. "Hardly."

"Your turn," he says.

"Um, for what?"

"Time to tell me everything that happened at work with Jimmy. If you were able to go to HR and file a formal complaint, *something* had to have happened."

I hem and haw, unwilling to talk about it, but gradually Tony worms the whole story out of me. By the time I get to the end, he's put his pizza down and become stiff on the couch.

"Did he abuse you, Heather, sexually?"

The question takes me by surprise. I'd never thought of Jimmy or what we did together that way. "I don't think so, at least not how you mean."

"How was it then?" His voice is low, with a steel edge to it. "It sounds like he forced you to do things you didn't like."

"Not really. I mean, it wasn't always like that. I'm not an idiot, Tony. He just got a little carried away... and maybe he wasn't always so concerned with whether or not I was as 'into' it as he was."

Tony stares at me, his gaze intense and heavy. "That night, last week... in your kitchen when I cooked for you... and you...did you..." He looks away, then back to me, as if he's steeling himself for bad news. "Did you feel I was too forceful when I held your head? Did I go too far?"

I climb across the couch and into his lap, pulling the blanket up around my shoulders to lock the warmth in. "Look at me, Tony." His eyes meet mine, the emotion I see nearly clogs my throat. "Do I behave like a meek and cowed woman?"

Tension eases out of him. "No."

"Did I, in any way, seem like I was not having a damn good time *any* of the times we've been together?"

He smiles, his rakish good humor coming back. "Nope. Never."

"Then there's your answer." I snuggle into his chest, happy when his arms come around me. "I was a different person with Jimmy. I didn't know myself. I only knew I didn't want to be alone for the rest of my life... and that led to me taking more shit than I bargained for."

His lips press against my hair. "I'm so punching that asshole if I ever meet him."

"Fine by me. Might knock some sense into him."

"I highly doubt that. Assholes like him will always exist."

I cringe inwardly, thinking about Tammy and how nice she is. I'll have to say something to her before it's too late. I sigh, this one not of contentment, but rather in annoyance over a difficult task to come.

"So tell me, besides the Jimmy problem, how do you like your new job?"

I shrug, realize that's not really an answer and shift to the side so I can respond while considering his question. "It's okay. Nothing exceptionally glamorous or anything. Same thing I've done for years, only this time with a title and more pay. I mean, when it gets right down to it, it's a corporate job. You know what that's like."

"Yeah, I do. Been there, done that. Glad to be done with it." His warm hand slides over my thigh, not sexually, more in comfort. "I just hoped for more for you."

"Me? How much better can it get? I'm twenty-eight and the CFO. Granted, I worked my way to the job, rather than was interviewed and hired for it, but I'm not going to quibble." I smile to show I am happy, but strangely enough, I know what Tony means. A corporate job pays the bills, but it leaves a lot to be desired regarding making you feel fulfilled in life.

"What about your hobby—photography. You're really, really good. Have you thought about pursuing that as a career?"

I shrug both shoulders. "I dunno. I never really thought about it. Photography was more of a pipe dream in high school and college." I think about all the classes I took, and the fact I never really pursued it outside of a course and my own personal time. "Well, that's not really true either. I mean, sure I've always enjoyed it... but it never really occurred to me as viable *career*, you know? Way too many starving artists out there in the world."

"What if you could? I mean, if money wasn't a concern?"

I shove further away so I can get a good look at his face. "Are you suggesting what I think you are?" My tone becomes heated. "I have no intention of becoming a kept woman who needs a man to support her."

"Slow down there, Ms. Feisty," he smiles to show he knows he's using the same term to describe me as Jimmy did in the lobby. "I'm not offering to support you." He squeezes my thigh once more. "Although... I might be tempted to literally support you in various sexual positions." He winks. "Just think on it."

I nudge his shoulder. "I'm serious, Tony. I have money saved, but I'm not interested in taking a risk like that right now, not when I'm in a good place at work."

"How about if an art gallery owner really liked your work and wanted to show it?"

I freeze, staring at his light brown eyes to see if he's funning with me. "Really? You shared my work with someone and they liked it?" At his slow smile I sit up straighter on the couch. "You're not teasing?"

"I'm not teasing if you're not annoyed I did it without asking. If you are, then yes, I'm totally teasing."

"Oh my God! What did they say?"

"*He* said you had an incredible eye. Loved your city shots and your model ones. Wants to do a showing."

"I can't believe it!" I squeal in excitement, bouncing on the couch and losing the blanket. "You even showed him the ones of you?" I freeze again, my body going from hot to cold so quick I feel like a crazy person. "Wait, he thought you were a model. He didn't see your face?"

"I did some creative cropping. The software I got is really incredible."

I jump up, the excitement not letting me stay still a moment longer. "I can't believe this! That's incredible. I don't know what to say. Yes, I do. Wow! This is so awesome!"

I leap on Tony, plastering his face with kisses. "You've got to be the most incredible man in the world. Who does this kind of thing?" My mind races with the possibilities. Will people like my work or will it be hum-drum, like it's nothing special? Oh my God, what will I do if people don't come? That would be way worse.

Tony chuckles. "You've got a cute little crease between your eyebrows. Your mind must be generating problems." He hugs me, lending me his warmth and unconditional support. "Don't stress, Heather. This should be something to celebrate."

"It is, don't get me wrong. There's just so many possibilities. Could go well, could be a phenomenal failure... Oh God." I clutch my stomach. "I think I may get sick."

"Relax." His hands shift me to the side, perhaps worried I may indeed puke on him. "It'll go fine. I'm sure people will love your work. You should see the finals I printed and sent. Really gorgeous."

"Oh my God—you sent them already? When is the showing?"

"As it happens, the gallery had a mess up with a shipment and had to cancel the showing planned for this weekend. Francesco asked if we could put you in last minute and I said I'd check with 'the artist' to confirm."

"This weekend? Today is Wednesday. That's no time to prep."

"Oh, you mean like ads and announcements? I already put a call in to the paper. They were very interested to hear about a 'local artist Tony Carmine discovered.' If you agree, they'll run a piece in the society pages mentioning the show. And running ads is easy. Copy can be written and submitted asap."

"I-I don't know what to say. This is all happening so fast. This is incredible."

Tony reaches for me, pulling me onto his lap. "Say yes, darlin'. Take a risk. Live a little."

I take a shaky breath, unwilling to process everything he's thrown at me in the past five minutes. But one thing is for sure, I can do anything with him by my side. "Yes. I'll do it." My stomach clenches. "And if I throw up and humiliate myself, it's all on you."

He laughs once more and gently kisses me. "How about we go a day early for you to check over the exhibit and get a lay of the land." My lover smiles and touches his forehead to mine. "If you feel you need some strategically placed trash cans added we can have Francesco add them."

I nod, unwilling to trust my mouth to speak. I'm overwhelmed by his generosity and sincerity. My heart swells in my chest. I can't believe how much I love this man, how much he's come to mean to me in such a short span of time. I'm so afraid something will happen to ruin this for me.

I swallow down the bile, refusing to let my fears rule me. This is an amazing opportunity. I will not self-sabotage it with my old insecurities.

Chapter Twenty

The next two days go by in a blur of work and preparation. I stayed both nights at Heather's so I could better handle the minute details for the showing. Despite my offhanded comments to Heather, there are a lot of tiny things to iron out, but I'm doing them all myself so she can focus on work.

She's been a hot mess since Wednesday night. I probably should have picked a better time to ask her to dinner at my mom's on Sunday. She said yes, and seemed happy, but she threw up twice before settling down to sleep. She insisted it was over the showing, not meeting my mom, and I believe her.

I hadn't anticipated she'd react so strongly with nerves. It makes my nice surprise seem more painful than good. She keeps assuring me it's fabulous, but at times I see her with a look of sheer panic on her face and wonder if I did the right thing.

I was there when she called Carla with the news, and by the squeals heard over the phone, it's safe to say she's excited about the showing, too. They've invited all their yoga buddies, and one of the Parkerson executives saw the piece in the paper, so it looks like she'll get some support from work relationships, too.

I've planned a private dinner for the two of us at the gallery tonight. She still hasn't seen the work Francesco and I have picked, and I want her to see it as her friends and prospective buyers will on Saturday night. He and I spent time going over contact sheets and selecting more images. Heather will have close to sixty prints on display. An incredible number for a new artist on the scene. We lucked out Francesco had the room for it.

Sometimes, timing is everything in life.

Well—connections, preparedness, and sheer luck play a good part of it, too.

"How do I look?" Heather asks, twirling in an outfit I've never seen. She's wearing an emerald sheath dress that ends at her knees, the jewel tone showing off her black hair and creamy skin. Makes me wish we were staying in so I could peel it off her... with my teeth.

I whistle low. "Like a million bucks. Is this for tonight or tomorrow?"

"For tonight. Carla helped me pick something even fancier for tomorrow." She presses a hand to her stomach. "Oh God, maybe eating isn't such a good idea."

I take her in my arms and hold her close, running my hands down her back to cup her ass and haul her close. "You'll do fine, don't worry. I'll be right by your side." I lean in to kiss her, a soft brush of the lips. "Tonight is just for us. No one will be there except the owner, and he'll leave after he lets us in."

She nods, pinning a brave smile in place. "I'm sure I'll do fine."

Close to seven o'clock we leave, the hired car waiting downstairs to take us to the gallery downtown. On the ride over we're quiet, each lost in our own thoughts.

Tonight is the big night. For me that is. I'm going to take the plunge and say it first. I plan to tell her I love her when we're all alone. I don't want it confused with the excitement of tomorrow. Saturday night is all for her. And if she does get sick during the exhibit, I'm sure she'd appreciate me not springing something else major on her, too.

Heather squeezes my hand again. "This is all so... unreal. I still can't believe it's happening."

I smile to reassure her, unwilling to say more until we get there. I'm sure she'll be as impressed with her work on display as the gallery staff were. Very soon, we pull up to the curb. She squeaks when the door opens, then gulps air like a gasping fish when I hand her out of the car.

I run a hand down her back. "Deep slow breaths, hon. You'll do fine. No one is here but us."

"And Francesco. Does he know I'm your girlfriend? Does that look bad? Like I had to sleep with you to get you to support my art?"

I stifle a chuckle, unsure how she'll react to my humor at her expense. "Yes, he knows we're dating. He wanted to know my involvement and how I had access to your work. You'll need to sign some paperwork tomorrow so he can handle sales and commission."

She nods, staring through the glass at the work on display—none of it hers, but I'm sure she's wondering what it would be like to have her work in the front windows.

I open the door, motioning for her to proceed me. "And no, there was no mention of my sleeping with you to support your work. After all," I say with a smile, "it's not like I have a rep in the art world for 'discovering' new talent. Like I told you, he's an old friend, all I did was ask if he could look at it. The rest was all him."

"Buonasera!" A robust Italian-accented voice calls good evening to us. The smartly dressed Francesco enters the foyer, hands extended in greeting. "Is this delicate flower the talented artist?" Typical suave salesman, he glides over to us fawning over Heather. "Only one so beautiful could capture such emotion and depth behind the lens." He kisses both her cheeks and then stands back to admire her more.

"Thanks again, Francesco. And yes, this is Heather." I make quick introductions and he motions for us to follow him into the next room, reserved for paintings and sculpture.

"Your gallery is impressive, sir. Thank you so much for agreeing to show my work."

He beams under her compliment, but waves her words off with a hand. "It is your Tony here who saved me. I had another artist scheduled, but last minute the shipment didn't arrive. Your work fit in perfectly." He continues to a second room. "Come, come. Tony tells me this is the first time you'll see some of the work mounted and framed."

Heather nods, slowing her step to pause on the threshold. A large, well lit room expands before us. Spotlights shine on each individual print, showcasing the shadows and highlights in each one. Some of them look like you could walk right into the print. To the left are all her Manhattan and Hoboken shots, and to the right, and dead center in the room, are all the ones she took of me last week. A small table for two is arranged in the center of the space, set up with the meal I had delivered and a wine bucket close by with champagne on ice.

Her breath catches in her throat. "It... It's indescribable. I never dreamed..." She strolls in, staring at the largest picture of me. The chains are draped over my shoulders, the afternoon light casting warmth and mystery on the glossy paper. "Just gorgeous," she whispers. "It's hard to believe I took them."

Francesco chuckles. "You better have or I could get in a lot of trouble trying to sell someone else's work."

Heather whips around, horror on her face. "I swear, they're mine. I just meant..."

I place a hand on her shoulder and squeeze. "Relax, hon. He's joking."

"I'll leave you two in peace. You can lock up, Tony?"

"No problem."

"Come, follow me out. You'll drop the keys off with security next door when you're done."

I look to Heather, who nods, assuring me she's fine while I escort Francesco out.

"Thanks again for letting us have the place to ourselves for an hour or so. I really appreciate it."

"No problem. Most artists have a small gathering the night before for friends and such." We walk to the front foyer where he points out the keys. "You're not planning something big and private are you?" He raises eyebrows. "Like a proposal?"

"No, but thanks for making me feel like I should have." I smile. "Maybe next time."

"Hmmph. No romance these days. Everyone rushes." He turns to the door and hesitates. "Who is this? A friend who's joining you two for dinner?"

I grab the keys and look up, my breath caught in my throat. It's Portia. "Ah... not really." I step forward and open the door to let her in, warning her with my eyes to be quiet. "I'll see her out in a few minutes, Francesco. Thanks again, and we'll see you tomorrow night."

He makes his goodbyes and exits, leaving me alone with Portia in the vestibule of the gallery. I wait 'til he's out of sight to say anything, my voice coming out in a low whisper. "What brings you here, Portia? How did you find me?"

"You're not the only one who can hire a private detective." Her eyes glitter with malice. "Imagine my surprise when I found out you were seeing someone else." She pushes past me and rushes toward the first gallery room. "Is she here? The newspaper said your art showing was for a Heather Pierce? Since a private showing would be the night before, I went on a hunch you'd be here." She looks around, eyeing up the other doorways leading off the room. "I'd like to meet the woman who's snagged your attention. Or at least snagged it for now."

I follow her, wishing I could strangle her and toss her body in the alley.

Temper, temper. What happened to the supportive moron who's ready to be a father?

Before I have a chance to respond, Heather strides out from the second gallery. "I'm Heather. Is there something I can help you with?"

Portia eyes the other woman slowly, from head to toe. "Well, well... if it isn't the latest catch of the week. According to the man I hired, she's the third one you dated after me. Does she know about *us* yet?"

I move to Heather's side, ignoring the growing sense of dread in my gut, silently letting Portia know with my actions who's more important to me. "There is no 'us', Portia. There's you and your current situation. Which we still have no proof is connected to me."

She waves a hand away, like the detail of the DNA test is insignificant. "I may have been a party girl, but I know who I slept with in the time frame the doctors say I conceived." Her eyes narrow on Heather. "Has he told you we're having a baby together?"

The shock she was hoping for doesn't happen, as Heather responds in stride, "Oh, you mean the baby *you're* having, the one you *hope* is Tony's? Let's just wait and see how the test comes out at the twenty week mark, shall we?"

"Well, well, well. Isn't this just adorable?" She speaks to me, ignoring Heather. "You found someone you can *talk* to. Bully for you. I should have known there was a reason you didn't want to give us a shot again. Why couldn't you have just told me yourself?"

I step toward Portia, hoping to usher her toward the door, but seeing the determined look on her face I doubt I'll be very successful. "I was a complete jerk when you told me. I'll own up to that. I never told you about Heather because it didn't relate to what happened with you and me. Whether you like it or not, I don't have feelings for you. What happened between us is the *past,* Portia. You'll do better to accept that and move on." I reach for her arm, hoping I can gently steer her out, only to have her twist out of my grasp.

"Not so fast there, Tony." Her gaze settles on Heather and my blood starts to boil. I won't allow her to hurt the woman I love. "Are you going to stick around for the twenty week mark, sugar?" Portia smirks, an evil look on her face. "How about the full nine months to see the beautiful baby? You may be here now, but are you in it for the late night feedings?" Her lips turn up in a derisive snarl. "You gonna change my baby's diapers for Tony?"

Heather walks closer and stands next to me. Her hand links with mine and grips hard. "I'm in it for the long haul, Portia. So you better get used to seeing my face."

Portia's expression turns bitter. "Yeah, until he gets tired of you. Just like he did me." Having spewed enough drama, she turns and stalks out, leaving the gallery.

I squeeze Heather's hand and let go, then march to the door to lock it behind the hormone-crazed woman.

I return to where we were standing and take the slim woman in my arms, noting she's no longer shaking from nerves like she was when we came in. "I'm sorry about that. If I'd known she was going to pull something like this I would have warned you—or, I dunno, planned something else." I sigh and hold her close. "Please don't let her ruin this experience for you."

"Me? Don't you worry about me, Tony. You've got your hands full with that one. I don't envy you."

"With any luck, the baby won't be mine."

Heather leans back to look into my face "She mentioned a detective. I take it you've hired one, too?"

I nod. "I'd hoped to dig up other potential fathers."

"Any luck?"

"Unfortunately... no. She dated a couple of other guys, but nothing concrete has come up." Tension courses through me and I feel like punching a wall. This totally sucks. All of it. But I've got to let it go. There are some things in life that just are, and this is one of them.

"Tony?"

"Yeah?"

"I'm here. I'll be here. She won't drive me away and neither will a baby."

"I hope so. It's a lot to ask of someone, I know."

"I mean it, mister." She stands on her toes and kisses me. "I'm in for the long haul." She tugs my hand and leads me back to the gallery showcasing her art. "Look at what you've done for me. I mean it—look, you fool." She motions around the room with her arms, then turns back to me. "No one has believed in me like you, no one but my parents. You've supported me through a situation that could have lost you your job, bought me a fancy camera so I could pursue a passion, cheered me on when I tackled a new position at work, built me a freakin' studio in your apartment, and then you've gone and done—" She sweeps an arm behind her. "This!"

I smile at her enthusiasm, pleased she's so happy, deciding it's a good time to come clean about everything. "And then there's the car..."

"You mean the car you lent me? Holy crap, Tony! What did you do?"

"Well, I did mention that Gino owns a car dealership... so, I may have purchased a demo car in your name..."

"No way!" She launches herself at me, wrapping her arms around my neck. "Tony! You are too much!"

I hold her close and breathe in her scent, grateful she's not mad. "What's the point of having all this money if you can't do something nice for the person you..."

She stills in my arms. "The person you... what?"

I stare into her dark as sin eyes and leap off the abyss. "For the person you love." My mouth finds hers and I pour my desire for her into the kiss.

Chapter Twenty One

Heather

As his mouth moves over mine, there's a wrenching in my chest. This is it. This is love. The big showy emotion so many of us are afraid of, and yet the elusive one so many of us seek.

I knew I felt it for him, but I wasn't sure if he felt the same way, so I held back. Not a lot, but enough to protect my heart should he decide he'd lost interest.

"I could never lose interest in you." Oh my God, I must have said that last bit out loud. "You're the bravest —most incredible—woman I've ever met." He reaches a hand down and cups my ass in his palm. "You've made me a better man. I don't ever want to let you go."

I resist hiking a leg up around his waist and grinding against him, but just barely. "You..." my breath pants out, heart pounding like I've sprinted a mile. "You're amazing."

Tony eases me away from his front, his erection clear behind the fabric of his fly. "I'm pretty sure Francesco has cameras in here. We may want to tone it down."

"Wait 'til I get you home, mister."

Despite our blossoming love choking the air, and the giddy, stupid smiles neither of us can hide, we manage to eat the meal Tony arranged and then slowly peruse all the photographs on display—all while sipping champagne. It was simply mind-blowing. Tomorrow is going to be a night like no other. Geez, *tonight* is already a night like no other. Seems like we're experiencing lots of firsts together. And what could be better?

Tomorrow night, my work will be on display in a gallery—a gallery in Manhattan no less. I never would have dreamed such a thing could happen. I never would have thought my work was worthy if it wasn't for Tony. A hobby. One I have a passion for, sure. But good enough that people wanted to buy it? Unreal.

And judging by the high price tags, which Tony assured me is really not too high for a print, it looks like Francesco believes in my work, too. What will my friends and co-workers say tomorrow? How will the patrons of the gallery receive it? I'll find out soon. And with luck, maybe we'll spend most of the time between now and then naked so I won't have to think about it too much. My vomiting the other night was embarrassing. I've come so far and grown so much, it felt like the old, post-Jimmy Heather rather than the current me.

But no more. I'm not the insecure woman who did whatever her boyfriend wanted just to keep him happy. Now I'm the woman who embraces her sexuality and goes after what she wants. If I'm occasionally derailed by bouts of anxiety and fear, I'm still a stronger woman than I ever was before meeting Tony.

I'm keenly aware neither of us has actually uttered the three little words *I love you*, yet, but maybe we can rectify that tonight when our clothes come off and we have a chance to express how we feel physically—which always seems easier for me. The unexpected clash with Portia is behind us and nothing stands in the way of enjoying the rest of the evening alone.

We take a cab back to my place, both of us too eager to wait for a hired car. Tony's palm locks to mine as the elevator ascends, and I swear my heart feels like it's going to beat right out of my chest. His thumb caresses the back of my hand, making me hyper-aware of the handsome man standing next to me.

"Is it me," I venture in a hushed tone, "or does it feel like the first time all over again?"

Tony chuckles, low and masculine, causing my toes to curl in my heels. "If I'm remembering correctly, we were both racing to get here after sexting each other at work." The doors open and he tugs me into the hall. "I'd say this instance will be even better."

He uses his key to unlock my door and a warm feeling cascades through me. It's the first time we've arrived here together where he's used his key to get in. It feels really nice, like he's always belonged here.

Once the door closes, Tony leans me against it, cradling my cheeks in his hands. My breath hitches as he lowers his mouth to mine. The soft tenderness of his lips feels like a tease, enticing me with the heat I know he has banked below the surface. The same heat I have for him.

I reach up and run my fingers through his hair, twining them through the soft strands and tugging, drawing him closer for more pressure. Chocolate and champagne linger in his mouth, driving me to suck and pull his questing tongue deeper. A murmur of appreciation sounds deep in his chest, encouraging me to go further.

Right as I slide a hand down to cup his growing erection, his phone rings.

I pull back and look into his eyes. "Are you going to answer it?"

He grunts and reaches to pull me closer. "No."

It rings again.

Gratitude washes through me. This is the man who, a little over a month ago, couldn't live without his damn phone. But still, I resist his advance. I'm curious. "It's after ten. On a Friday. Could it be one of your brothers?"

It rings again. "Don't care," he says, stepping near, trying to recapture my mouth.

I evade him and laugh. "Aren't you even going to look?" It's amazing how I have no lingering fear or doubt, that even if it is an old fling calling for a booty call he wouldn't care.

He sighs heavily, acting all put out. "All right. I'll look." Tony checks the screen and his face falls. "It's

Portia. And I did promise I wouldn't dodge her calls anymore."

I'm a little annoyed at myself for pushing him to check and secretly hope she doesn't abuse his promise too much in the future.

"Hello?" he pauses for a second, his face creasing with worry. "Okay, calm down. I'll meet you at the hospital. Which one are you going to?" He nods while listening. "Try not to panic. Can you get there on your own?" He looks to me, concern in his eyes. "Trust them, they know what they're doing."

He hangs up the phone. "Portia's bleeding. She called an ambulance. They're taking her to the hospital."

"An ambulance? Is it that bad?"

Tony shrugs. "I'm not sure. She's scared and doesn't have a fast way there. I don't blame her for not wanting to take a cab. I've got to go. She thinks something may be happening with the baby." He runs a hand over his head, looking a little lost. "Will you come with me?"

"Of course." The answer leaps to my lips without any hesitation. I may not be happy about another woman having his baby, but I'd never leave his side when he needs me.

We arrive and they tell us nothing. We're not technically family, so I understand, but it's not easy. It's much harder for Tony to sit and wait. I see the old executive authority rolling off him, demanding to break free and insist on an update. The doctors come and go, but reveal nothing, not even acknowledging we're there. Then again, it's late on a

Friday night. I'm sure they're busy due to the craziness of the weekend.

After two hours, we're allowed in to see Portia, at her request. She's crying, tears streaming down her face while she sits in the hospital bed, all alone, no supportive parents in sight. My gut twists at her obvious grief.

Now is not the time for petty differences, and Tony looks like he has no idea what to do. I rush forward and take her hand, "Are you okay?"

She nods, looks down at our clasped hands and squeezes my hand in return. "Thanks. I wasn't sure if you'd come. I'm glad you did."

Tony stands beside me, uncertainty in his face. "Is the baby okay? Did they stop the bleeding?"

I resist stomping on his foot. He really is a clueless guy sometimes.

A laughing sob escapes the shattered woman. "There is no baby."

"Portia, I'm so sorry," I say, reaching out and rubbing her upper arm.

She wipes her eyes and nose with her free hand. "Funny thing, you sound like you mean it."

"I do. I'd never wish a miscarriage on anyone."

She drops my hand and reaches for the box of tissues near her hip. After blowing her nose, she says, "Turns out there never was a baby."

Tony tenses beside me.

Unsure what will come out of his mouth, I ask, "What do you mean? Didn't you have a positive blood test?"

Portia nods. "I did. When I arrived, the bleeding was light. The doctors first said if they could get it to stop I might be okay. Then they did an ultrasound to check and make sure the baby was okay. That's when they told me there was no embryo. I was never pregnant in the first place."

"How could that be?" Tony asks, genuine concern in his tone. "I saw the test. Your blood had enough growth hormone in it to indicate a healthy first trimester pregnancy."

"Some such shit called a 'blighted ovum.' My body thought it was pregnant and acted like I was. Gestational sac, growth hormones, everything. But no baby." Tears pour anew down her face. "At first, I wasn't so sure I wanted to be pregnant. But I'd come to terms with it, you know?" She grabs more tissues.

Tony reaches out and takes her hand. "Yeah, I do know. I'm really sorry, Portia."

"I wasn't trying to trap you, Tony. I just didn't want to face the future on my own."

My heart hurts, witnessing her sadness. I may not have liked her, but she didn't deserve this.

"You wouldn't have been alone." He says softly. My heart hurts at the loss I hear in both their voices. "I would have helped with the baby."

She sniffs loudly. "Oh God, this is so much harder than I bargained for. I wasn't ready to be a mom. But now I don't even have a chance to change."

Tony squeezes her hand before letting go. "You already have."

We stay with her a while, until Tony convinces her to call her parents. Even though the baby crisis is past she should still talk to them and let them help her when she needs it.

Once her folks arrive, we leave. The journey back to my place is silent. Neither of us ready to talk after the emotionally draining experience. A part of me wants to climb into bed and pull the covers high, shutting out the rest of the world for a while, but another part of me feels restless, too.

When we enter my apartment I go straight the kitchen, needing to be doing something.

"Coffee?" I ask while getting out the supplies.

"Thanks."

In a few minutes the coffee is brewing and the air fills with the rich aroma. I move to Tony and lean into his chest, wrapping my arms around his waist.

"I'm not sure what to say."

He sighs and surrounds me with his arms. "Me either. I feel sorry for Portia. And I'm ashamed of the relief I feel."

"I understand. I feel the same way." I lean back to peer up at his face. He looks haggard and tired. "Think she'll be okay?"

"I don't know. I hope so. Her parents seemed concerned and supportive when they got there. I'm sure they'll help her through it."

"Should we check on her? You know, in a week or so?"

He sighs, sounding like a weight is on his chest. "I have no idea. I guess a phone call would be the right thing to do."

I nod.

"You were great, by the way." He kisses me on the forehead. "Thanks."

"Me? I didn't do anything."

"You were decent to her, which is more than she expected. I saw the surprise on her face."

I shrug, uncomfortable with the praise when it was the right thing to do. "I'm sure she would have done the same for someone else."

"I doubt it... but she might now."

We fix our coffee and move to the couch, Tony pulling the blanket over our legs.

"How are you doing?" I ask, draping my legs over his. "And I mean really doing. You seemed to have come to terms with the possibility of a baby... and now it's gone."

"I feel..." he shrugs. "I'm not sure. Years ago I thought I didn't ever want to become a father. Now... now it seems like an idea I could look forward to."

Warmth swells inside me. If anyone had told me a jet-setting playboy would turn around to be such a decent, stand-up guy, I would never have believed them. If I hadn't witnessed his growth firsthand I would have brushed it off as hearsay. Tony has become a man any woman would be honored to have at her side.

Tony runs a warm hand over my thigh. "And now we've got a gallery showing and dinner with my mom to look forward to. Aren't you lucky?"

"I am lucky. I'm a little panicky, too. Will your brothers come to the showing tomorrow, so at least I'm not meeting everyone for the first time on Sunday?"

Tony nods, his hot palm settling very close to the juncture between my thighs. "I'm sure they'd both like to come. Work might get in the way for Vinnie, we'll see. They only had great things to say about the prints they saw."

"They didn't tease you about the risqué ones?"

"Not really." Tony raises a shoulder, expressing unconcern. "I'm sure they'll wait for an audience to really lay it on."

We cuddle in silence on the couch, tension from the night easing out of both of us little by little as we enjoy the coffee.

"Thank you for tonight," Tony says. "I really appreciate you coming with me and standing by my side. It means a lot to me."

I sip my coffee and smile. "You're welcome. You mean a lot to me, too."

He takes my mug and sets it and his own on the coffee table. "That's it, huh?" There's a twinkle in his eye. "I 'mean a lot to you'?"

"I... uh..."

He kisses me, long and deep and sensuous. He moves us, repositioning me on the couch so he leans over me, pinning me beneath him. "Cat got your tongue?" he smiles, then leans in to kiss my neck. "I know how you feel. Don't hide from me."

A little *eep* of sound escapes as he nips under my ear. "I don't know what you're talking about."

His head whips up and he laughs at the faux innocent expression on my face. "Little minx." He thrusts his hips forward, grinding his growing erection into my middle. "You sure do know what I'm talking about."

His lips return to mine, insistent and persuasive, nibbling on my bottom lip and then licking lightly. A soft moan of want escapes me and he smiles against my mouth. He shifts his weight to the side and runs a possessive hand across my breasts, then trails lower to my abdomen, and beyond, hesitating over the heat between my thighs.

"You want me to take this dress off you, don't you?" he whispers, nuzzling my cheek, while lifting his hot hand away.

In answer, my hips arc off the couch, seeking his touch once more. I stare into his caramel eyes, my voice hitching with desire. "I want more than just that, Tony."

"Tell me," he whispers, trailing his palm up my thigh under my dress.

"I want you in my arms, all night, making me feel like there's no other man in the world."

There's a devilish glint in his eye. "And why would you want that?"

The words struggle to break free, barreling past every fear I've ever had. "Because I love you. And you're the only man for me."

His hand cups me over my underwear. "Now see? Was that so hard?"

I chuckle, a low throaty sound, as I reach to massage him between his legs. "There's certainly something hard right here."

A shudder ripples across his frame, "Woman, what you do to me."

"Hmmm... do tell."

The tenderness in his eyes makes my breath catch in my throat. "I'll sum it up with three little words—I love you."

I may not know what tomorrow holds. But one thing I know for sure. This man will have a place in my heart forever.

~~*~~

About the Author

C.J. Ellisson lives in northern Virginia with her husband, two children, three dogs, and a fluffy black cat who makes her sneeze. Unlike most full-time authors, she's also battling severe chronic illness. C.J. works daily to put her Lupus into remission and continues to fight numerous bacterial infections while her immune system slowly attacks her body. She turned to writing when she could no longer work outside the home and claims the escape of penning contemporary erotic romance, urban fantasy, and erotica has helped save her sanity.

Vanilla Twist is the third published book in the *Walk on the Wild Side* series and there are currently five novels (three for Heather and Tony) and two novellas planned.

Titles in reading order:
Heather and Tony's Books
Vanilla on Top
Vanilla Twist
Vanilla Spice (release date late 2014)

Best Friend Books
Avoiding Mr. Right (Carla's story)
Loving Ms. Wrong (Marcus's story, a novella in the *Girls Night Out, Volume 2* anthology)

Andrea's story (no title yet) will be written after *Vanilla Spice* is completed and there may be books for Tony's brothers if there is enough reader interest.

Books in C.J.'s erotic urban fantasy series, *The V V Inn:*

Full Length Novels:
Vampire Vacation, Book 1
The Hunt, Book 2
Big Game, Book 3
The V V Inn eBook Bundle, Books 1-3 (best price!)

Novellas:
Death Times Two, Book 3.5
Death's Servant (Jon's tale, First Prequel Novella)

Join C.J. Ellisson's Monthly Newsletter to Receive Notice of:

~ Contests
~ Free Reads & Sneak Peeks
~ Book Signing & Appearances
~ Online Reader Events
~ Upcoming Sales
~ New Releases

To sign up, copy and paste this site address into your browser's address bar: bit.ly/cj-news

MORE places to connect with C.J.:

Website: cjellisson.com
Facebook: facebook.com/C.J.EllissonFanPage
Street Team: facebook.com/groups/cjeseethe

Do you miss signed books? C.J. offers free, full-color signed 4x6 postcards of all her novels to readers who've left honest reviews on any retailer or book reviewing website. To obtain yours, please email your review URLs to admin@cjellisson.com with your mailing address—international readers welcome!